Born in California ~~...~~ n now a teacher in t ~~...~~ at the age of seven – ~~...~~ he family of ducks who lived in the ~~pond~~ ~~...~~ ~~...~~ ting ever since.

My husband and I are lucky enough to have two smart, wonderful children who live on opposite coasts of the US. Since I've become a HarperImpulse author, my remaining daydream is to live in Paris or London.

www.nancyhollandwriter.com
@nancyholland5

Found: One Secret Baby

NANCY HOLLAND

A division of HarperCollins*Publishers*
www.harpercollins.co.uk

Harper*Impulse* an imprint of
HarperCollins*Publishers*
1 London Bridge Street
London SE1 9GF

www.harpercollins.co.uk

A Paperback Original 2016

First published in Great Britain in ebook format by Harper*Impulse* 2016

A catalogue record for this book
is available from the British Library

ISBN: 9780008206741

Set in Minion by Palimpsest Book Production Ltd, Falkirk, Stirlingshire

Printed and bound in Great Britain

MIX
Paper from
responsible sources
FSC™ C007454

For my beloved, patient husband.

Chapter One

The usual flicker of nerves made Rosalie Walker stand up straighter as the receptionist opened the door to show her visitor in. The appointment had been made this morning and she'd been too busy to Google this new client. Would Morgan Danby be a man or a woman?

She looked up, far up, into blue eyes fringed with thick, black lashes.

Definitely a man. A man she could have sworn she'd dreamed about.

The spark of interest she saw in his eyes filled her mind with images of naked bodies intertwined on white sands along sun-sparkled seas. She allowed herself one second to feel like a woman before the lawyer took over.

She extended her hand. "Rosalie Walker." An involuntary purr shadowed her words.

But the spark in his eyes had burned itself out. He engulfed her hand in his, his no-nonsense expression just a step short of downright cold. "Morgan Danby."

His voice was deep, and as sexy as the rest of him, but like his face, it held no warmth. Only for that one moment had his eyes shown any sign of a flesh-and-blood man hidden behind the mask.

"Sit down, Mr. Danby." She gestured to the chair across the desk and sat in hers.

What would bring a gorgeous man in a hand-tailored suit and diamond cufflinks to a family law practice miles from Los Angeles' center of glamor and wealth?

"How can I help you?" The tell-tale purr lingered, but luckily he didn't seem to hear it.

"I'm here to learn more about the late Maria Mendelev."

The way he mispronounced Márya's name froze Rosalie's breath in her chest.

"What is your interest in the late Ms. Mendelev?" she managed in a neutral tone once her heart began to beat again.

He made a dismissive gesture with one aristocratic hand. "I'm not interested in her."

Anger closed Rosalie's throat, but she forced her lips to keep a smile of polite interest.

"I'm interested in the child she may have left behind."

The world spun away, then fell back into place on a less stable axis.

Rosalie fought to keep her eyes fixed on Mr. Danby's face without even a glance at the small photo stuck to the edge of her computer monitor.

"Wouldn't it make more sense to talk to the man who would be this supposed child's father?" Her voice sounded almost normal, but the rest of her body echoed with shock. "I understand he can be reached at San Quentin for the next thirty years or so."

"I've talked to him, but he insists he never got Ms. Mendelev pregnant."

It was hard to believe the man who murdered her friend would say the right thing for the right reason.

"Doesn't that settle the matter?"

Mr. Danby shook his head. "I suspect he's worried that if he admits he fathered a child, money will be taken out of his trust fund to support it."

2

That sounded more like her friend's killer.

"Why don't you contact Child Welfare Services?" Contempt colored her voice. "They would be responsible for a child with a deceased mother and an incarcerated father."

"It's unclear which county would be responsible for the child, given the Mendelev woman's wanderings in the last months before she died."

The Mendelev woman. How could he talk about Márya like that?

Rosalie stood up. "I don't think I can help you, Mr. Danby. I'm sure there are many other lawyers in Los Angeles who could find the information you want."

He looked up at her, one eyebrow raised. "You're the only lawyer who was a witness at the hearing on Ms. Mendelev's order of protection against her alleged abuser."

Rosalie closed her eyes against the mounting panic. Too much was at stake to let this man bait her into losing control. She put her hands on the desk and leaned into his personal space. The musky scent of his body distracted her for half an instant before she pushed it out of her mind.

"That 'alleged' abuser is the man who murdered her."

Something dangerous lit in Morgan Danby's dark blue eyes. Staying so close pushed Rosalie's courage to the limit. His gaze dropped to her breasts, now at his eye level. Her mind cringed, but she didn't move.

"He's also my brother," Danby said.

A burst of pure panic made her blink. The monster's family had finally shown up.

Morgan shifted in his chair. Claiming Charleston Thompson as a brother always made him feel as if he'd stepped in something vile.

The anger radiating from the woman who loomed over him didn't help. He might have found her attractive under other

3

circumstances. Brains always impressed him, although his tastes ran to tall, slender blondes, not chest-high brunettes with more attitude than charm.

He distracted himself from that inappropriate train of thought by glancing around the sleek, efficient office, straight out of a mid-range office-furnishings catalog.

Ms. Walker looked efficient too, but not quite as sleek. Wisps had escaped from the smooth cap of her hair to curl around her face, and a mysterious small white spot marred the shoulder of her suit jacket.

When she sank back into her chair, he could breathe more easily, but the flowery scent of her perfume lingered and kept his adrenalin, or some other stimulating hormone, at full force.

"I'm sorry to hear that," she said.

She was a cool one. Her face and body were frozen in the professionally appropriate attitude of polite attention. Only her fisted hands hinted at the anger he sensed boiling underneath the frosty façade, and she quickly dropped those to her lap, out of his sight.

An ice princess to match Lillian's ice queen. He wished he'd let his stepmother fight this battle for herself.

But he'd promised Lillian he would find her grandchild before Charlie's father did, and no small-time lady lawyer was about to freeze him out.

"Sorry my brother is a murderer, or sorry he's my brother?"

"Take your pick. You know him better than I do."

"You don't know him at all. But that didn't stop you from testifying against him."

"I didn't testify against him. I testified in support of Márya's— Ms. Mendelev's—petition for a court order to protect her from him."

Márya. That explained the brief flash of fire in those green eyes when he called the dead woman "Maria." But that was what Charlie called her. Why wouldn't he know how to pronounce

4

the woman's name? Given Charlie, he probably called her whatever he damned well pleased. "How long had you known her when you testified?" he asked

"About four months."

"That isn't very long to determine the dynamics of a violent relationship." The words left a nasty taste in his mouth, but he needed to break through Ms. Walker's icy façade.

"I determined that as soon as I saw her broken arm. The yellowed bruises from the last time he'd beaten her pretty much backed up that conclusion."

Morgan swallowed a bolt of anger at Charlie's brutality. "So you took it upon yourself to intervene."

"She begged me to help her."

The woman paused, but her face yielded no clue to what might be going on inside her head. She'd be murder to face in a courtroom, a talent clearly wasted in this one-step-up-from-a-storefront family law practice.

"And she was pregnant."

He allowed himself a thin smile. "So the investigator was right. There is a child."

Ms. Walker lowered her eyes to the desk and shook her head. "She was three months' pregnant and bleeding heavily."

Damn. How could he tell Lillian that Charlie had managed to kill his own kid?

Morgan took out his smartphone and opened a file. "What hospital did you take her to?"

Ms. Walker was still staring at the desk. "Merced County General." She spoke slowly, as if she needed to make an effort to remember, but that was ridiculous. All this had happened less than two years ago. Had her encounter with Charlie's lady friend really been that traumatic?

"Why there?"

Laser-green eyes snapped back to his, brown specks turned to gold. "I found Márya hiding in a campground at Yosemite, which is in Merced County. Since your brother forced her to quit school and her job when he invaded her life, she didn't have medical insurance."

"But she filed for the order of protection in Los Angeles County."

The tiniest shift in the woman's ramrod posture. What didn't she want him to know?

"It's easier to hide in L.A.," she said.

Rosalie hated to be reminded of those last months of Márya's life. Her friend had lived in constant fear that Charlie would find her. She'd moved every week from one homeless shelter to another. If only she'd accepted Rosalie's offer of a place to live until they got Márya's visa straightened out so she could get a job.

If only . . . The words echoed through the silence left behind by her friend's death.

Rosalie shook the memories off and refocused on the man who sat across from her.

How could Charlie Thompson have a brother who oozed wealth and power the way Morgan Danby did? Mr. Danby must have been four or five years younger than Charlie, and he didn't look at all like the stocky, red-haired murderer.

But her visitor had said something about a trust fund. And someone had had enough money to hire the best criminal defense lawyer in L.A. to represent Charlie. The investment had paid off. They'd plea-bargained down to life with the possibility of parole. The idea that Charlie would ever walk free again tightened Rosalie's stomach one more notch.

Another if only—if only she could have claimed attorney/client privilege and refused to answer Mr. Danby's questions. But she'd known from the start she couldn't be Márya's friend and her lawyer at the same time. And given her situation now, she didn't dare openly obstruct the efforts of Charlie's family to find out whether he had a child.

"Ms. Mendelev had no permanent address in Los Angeles," Mr. Danby said. "So apparently you weren't a good enough friend to give her a place to hide, as you put it, after she ended her relationship with my brother."

"Relationship?" Rosalie's temper finally snapped. "Like the one between a boxer and his punching bag?"

The corners of his mouth twitched. No doubt he was pleased he'd broken through her self-control. She softened her face to assume a professionally neutral expression again.

"I offered to let Márya live with me, but she was a proud woman. And once she had the protection order, she thought she'd be safe. Her attorney, the staff at the shelters where she lived, and I all tried to tell her otherwise, but in her home country defying a court order was something done only by the very brave or the very stupid." She paused. "Given how viciously he murdered a defenseless woman, I'd guess bravery isn't your brother's problem."

Mr. Danby had the decency to flinch. "I've read the police report on the incident."

She swallowed another jolt of anger. A woman's death was much more than an "incident." At least, it was in Rosalie's world. She wasn't so sure about Morgan Danby's.

"Where did you get your information?" she asked him.

"A private investigator."

Maybe she could use that somehow. "A private investigator who worked for you?"

He glanced away. "For my stepmother Lillian, Charlie's mother."

So this man didn't share a gene pool with Charlie Thompson. A tightness in her chest she'd scarcely been aware of loosened and she could breathe freely again.

"You must know it's not necessarily in the P.I.'s best interest to tell his client everything he knows." She let that sink in. "But it is in his interest to find leads he could be paid to follow."

She might have struck a nerve. After all, Mr. Danby was here

7

himself, which meant someone had had enough sense to fire the P.I. She'd bet it had been Danby.

"Why should I doubt the investigator's integrity?" he asked her in a slightly bored tone.

"Did he provide your stepmother with a copy of the coroner's report on Ms. Mendelev?"

Morgan Danby flinched again. "I assume the investigator didn't think that was something she needed to see."

"A smart move on his part. But you see my point."

"You're suggesting the P.I's claim that a child had survived was a ruse to squeeze more money out of Charlie's mother."

"Did he find any documentary evidence Ms. Mendelev had given birth?"

She held her breath, outwardly calm, inwardly hollow with fear.

Danby shook his head.

"The P.I. found a few people who thought she'd been pregnant when she'd arrived at the homeless shelter in Fresno, and one woman at an L.A. shelter who said she'd seen Ms. Mendelev with a baby shortly before Charlie . . . before she died."

"Staff members at the shelters or residents?"

"Residents. Staff members always claimed confidentiality when the P.I. talked to them."

"As they should, of course. They need to protect their clients from unwanted intrusions into their private lives." She gave him a pointed look, but he shook it off.

"Were Ms. Mendelev alive, I would have complete respect for her privacy."

Which probably meant he'd have refused to give Márya a dime of Charlie's money.

"But if she left a child behind," Danby continued, "well, of course, that child's grandmother has a keen interest in its welfare."

Rosalie couldn't stop another grimace at the "its", but emotion was her enemy here.

"The operative word being 'if.' Without any proof such a child exists, I hope you will do as you suggested and respect the late Ms. Mendelev's privacy."

"Of course." He stood up.

She stood too, but didn't extend her hand until he did, then shook his with a distaste she didn't bother to hide. "Goodbye, Mr. Danby."

"Goodbye, Ms. Walker. I won't say it's been a pleasure."

Under other circumstances, she might have smiled at that exit line. The man was witty as well as drop-dead sexy. He was also a major threat to everything that mattered in her life.

She showed him to the door, closed it behind him, and walked back to her desk on legs that barely held her. She sank gratefully into her chair, her whole body shaking.

After he left Rosalie Walker's office, Morgan did some quick research on his laptop at a nearby coffee house before he drove the rented Porsche past a house not far away.

Nothing unusual about the place or about anything he'd been able to dig up on the Walker woman, except that she owned the house free and clear. Given the location in a solidly middle-class L.A. neighborhood, it was hard to know how she'd managed to buy it without a mortgage. Maybe she'd inherited it. Or maybe she wasn't the one who'd paid for it.

Could the lady lawyer have a "sugar daddy," as his father would have said? For some reason the idea rankled. Still, it fit the contrast between the low-profile law practice and the high-priced house. She was an attractive woman, if you ignored the pit-bull personality, and she probably kept that leashed around the man who'd paid for the cozy little bungalow. If she did have a sugar daddy, though, it didn't look as if he lived in the house. Too many flowers in the garden. Two black-and-white cats lounged on the back of a flowered sofa in the front window. If Morgan didn't know better, he would have thought the house

9

belonged to some little old lady. But he'd spent an uncomfortable part of the afternoon trying not to stare at Ms. Walker's breasts, so he knew for a fact that she was no old lady.

He reminded himself he didn't like short, curvy women. Or lady lawyers. He especially didn't like lady lawyers he didn't trust.

Rosalie wasn't able to escape her office for another three hours. As she crossed the lobby on the way to the parking lot, she ran into her friend Vanessa, who was headed back in with a latte and muffin from the local coffee house.

Five-foot-ten and reed-thin, Vanessa could have been a supermodel, but she had a CPA along with her law degree and made her living in the arcane realm of tax law. Friends since college, for the last two years they'd shared an office suite, along with a receptionist and two paralegals, with three other solo-practice attorneys.

"Leaving early?" asked Vanessa. "Lucky you!"

Rosalie smiled. "I'm going home to my guy."

"Must be true love." Vanessa winked, took a sip of her coffee, and headed to her office.

Rosalie let herself into her elderly Saab and dumped her briefcase onto the passenger seat. Time to set aside the lawyer part of her life and focus on the part that made it all worthwhile.

Morgan Danby's face flashed across her mind, but she pushed the memory aside. His face may have stirred up a welter of half-forgotten longings, but she never wanted to see it again.

Ten minutes later she held the man in her life tight in her arms. Her eyes stung with tears of happiness as she kissed his cheek and felt his lips brush hers.

"Were you a good boy today?" she asked.

Joey blinked cornflower blue eyes at her and blew a soft raspberry.

Rosalie brushed a lock of strawberry blonde hair out of his chubby face and hugged his small body so tightly he tried to wiggle out of her arms.

Joey must have had a busy day at day care because he didn't indulge in his usual protest at being strapped into his car seat and fell asleep as soon as she started the engine. Which left her with nothing to do on the way home except think about Morgan Danby's visit.

She couldn't believe he hadn't questioned her more closely about how many months' pregnant Márya had been when they'd first met. Rosalie had never been a good liar because she rarely lied. She understood the power of truth.

Her mother had always told the truth about the long illness that had eventually taken her life. Her honesty had made it possible for Rosalie to trust that she always knew the worst. And that, in turn, had given her the strength to move beyond the slow tragedy playing itself out at home and thrive in the world.

She'd only lied today because she'd panicked, but it had worked. Nothing else mattered. Even her mother would have understood that.

Still, Rosalie wished she'd started adoption proceedings when she'd first gotten custody of Joey. She hadn't because it would have alerted Charlie's relatives to Joey's existence. She'd thought they wouldn't care enough to look for the boy, but she'd been wrong.

She glanced in the rearview mirror at the sleeping child who filled her life with such joy. She'd do whatever was necessary to protect him.

"I don't care what you have to do," Márya had told her right before she died, after she signed the papers giving Rosalie custody of her son, "Keep Joey away from Charlie's family."

Morgan raised his gaze from the laptop and looked down Wilshire Boulevard, the lights of Los Angeles nothing more than so many colored stars from the twentieth floor condo his company owned here. He took a sip of wine and rolled his shoulders.

When his smartphone beeped he made the mistake of checking to see who it was.

Lillian. He'd have to talk to her some time. Might as well do it now.

He saved the spreadsheet he was working on and answered on the second beep.

"Hello, Lillian. You're up late."

"Why didn't you call me with the report about your meeting with that woman who testified against Charleston?"

He swallowed the familiar irritation. "I told you I'd call when I learned something."

"You didn't learn anything at all about my grandchild?"

If she hadn't sounded more like a major general barking orders than a grieving grandmother, he might have had more sympathy for her.

"We're not sure there was . . . is a grandchild, remember? I have a couple of new leads to follow up, but nothing definite."

"This is taking too long. Are you sure we shouldn't have kept the private investigator?"

"We can always hire another P.I. if we need to." Preferably one smart enough not to try to bribe the bleeding-heart workers at some homeless shelter who'd not only refused to give him any information, but had also gotten his license suspended. Morgan disapproved of unethical behavior, but he could not tolerate stupidity.

"If you're sure." Lillian's voice sounded weary, older. "Call me if you learn anything."

"I will, but it may be a day or two. I have to drive up to Merced to check out those leads."

"Merced? Is that even in the United States?"

"Yes, it is. Good night, Lillian."

He needed to get this over with, and soon. Almost daily interaction with his father's second wife was not good for his mood.

She meant well—most of the time. But the woman pushed

12

buttons and pulled strings she probably had no clue were there. Every time he talked to her he felt drained afterwards, and vaguely angry. He sometimes wondered if his own mother would have had the same effect on him, if she'd bothered to stick around.

Morgan wished he could simply hire another P.I., but he couldn't shake the image of Charlie's child in some overcrowded foster home, subject to who knew what kind of abuse from the older kids. Kids could be cruel, especially if their victim couldn't fight back. And it was often easier for a paid caretaker to turn a blind eye than deal with bullying. He should know.

Besides, Morgan couldn't ignore the possibility that Charlie's father might locate the child first and claim custody. A judge could consider the elder Thompson's young new wife better mother material than Lillian, but two generations of abuse in the Thompson family was enough. More than enough.

Morgan pinched the bridge of his nose to forestall a headache that threatened to knock him off-task. Danby Holding Company needed his full attention if they were going to maximize their opportunities in this kind of market. He rolled his shoulders again and refocused on work.

Two days later Morgan understood the P.I.'s impulse to resort to bribery.

Death certificates were public records, but without a full name or date, the clerks couldn't tell him if such a record existed.

Medical records might be available to a family member, but since Charlie had never bothered to marry the Mendelev woman and there was no proof he was the father of any child she might have had, Morgan couldn't get anywhere near those records.

He was reduced to reading back copies of the Merced newspaper from the time when Charlie and the woman had lived in the area, but he found no mention of her or of any child. Only a paragraph about Charlie's arrest when he'd tried to break into the hospital to get at her.

When he called Lillian to say he'd hit a dead end, she was unconvinced.

"What about the woman lawyer?" his stepmother asked. "If she and that woman were such good friends, she should want to help you find my grandchild. We can offer the little darling a life someone like his mother could never have imagined. Far better than being in foster care with who-knows-what kind of people."

His thoughts exactly, but what more could he do?

"Lillian, I have a business to run. The same business that supplies most of your income. I don't have time for this wild goose chase. I need to get back to the office."

"I don't ask for much, after the years I spent raising you."

Paying other people to raise me, he corrected silently.

"But to have Charleston's child to love in my old age . . ." She gave an artful sniff.

He sighed. He hated it when she tried to play him like that, but she was the closest thing he had to a family, give or take a mother in Key West he hadn't seen or spoken to in almost thirty years.

"Okay. I'll talk to her." For some reason the idea of seeing Rosalie Walker again made him smile. "But don't get your hopes up. I doubt I'll learn anything new."

"I knew I could rely on you, Morgan. You were always such a good child."

I had to be or you might have walked out, the way my mother did. He ignored the little boy's voice inside him and resigned himself to a few days more in California.

Rosalie escaped the overheated courtroom and flipped open her phone. Her heart lurched when she clicked the calendar. Her appointments for the afternoon now included Morgan Danby.

The noisy courthouse lobby swirled around her with the same black panic that had almost overwhelmed her when Mr. Danby

14

first mentioned Márya's child. After three days, she'd thought the man was gone for good.

She sat down hard on a well-worn wooden bench and forced air into her lungs. Then she punched her office number and tried to act as if her world hadn't just been turned upside down—again.

"The judge is running late," she told her receptionist when he answered. "Please tell my afternoon appointments I'll be there as soon as I can, and reschedule anyone who can't wait."

And please, please make it so that Morgan Danby can't wait and can't reschedule, she added in silent prayer.

Not that she had much hope of that. For all his casual air, Mr. Danby didn't strike her as a man who would give up easily or be a gracious loser. But she had to win this one for Joey's sake.

When she reached her office building four hours later, the expensive black sports car in the parking lot warned her that her prayer had not been granted.

Mr. Danby stood in the reception area outside her office, staring at one of the paintings that decorated the wall, an impressionistic hibiscus in brilliant red with broad strokes of yellow, green, and black.

"Are you an art critic, Mr. Danby?" she asked, in lieu of the polite greeting she couldn't force out.

He scanned her wind-blown hairdo and crumpled linen suit. She ignored the urge to straighten herself the same way she'd ignored the flutter in her chest when she first saw him.

"Rough day in court?" he asked with one sexily raised eyebrow.

"Rough day on the freeway. I won in court."

"Congratulations." He turned back to the painting. "I didn't have a chance to look closely at this when I was here before. It's quite good. They both are." He gestured to the painting on the other wall, a golden poppy with the same bold strokes of contrast.

"Thank you."

"You painted them?"

15

She allowed herself a smile at his surprise. "My mother."

"She's very talented."

Her smile faded. "Was very talented. She's deceased."

"I'm sorry to hear that." His tone was more calculating than sympathetic.

"It's been a few years," she told him as she crossed to her office and gestured him in.

He gave the hibiscus another look before he followed her.

She went to her desk and set down the bag that held her tablet computer. Mr. Danby had his back to her, intent on the painting of a flower garden on the wall across from her desk.

"Your mother again?"

She nodded, fighting to ignore the tingle his gaze sent through her.

"And that one?" This time he pointed to the painting of a child in a sandbox that hung behind her. "Is that you?"

She refused to let him see the sudden flash of grief. "Yes."

"Your mother had a remarkable talent for that kind of middle-brow art."

Middle-brow art? Rosalie stiffened and gestured toward the chair across from her.

"Did she sell many of them?" He lowered his long, lean body into the chair.

Why should he care, if it was middle-brow art? She sat down and jiggled the mouse to turn on her computer monitor. "No. It was a hobby. She gave a few to friends."

He crossed his legs and leaned back to watch her face. "I came up blank in Merced."

Irritation morphed into dread. She sat up straighter and gave him an empty smile.

Chapter Two

The ice princess was back in place as soon as Morgan reminded Ms. Walker why he was here. He missed the very different, very attractive, person she had become when she smiled, but he couldn't undo what needed to be done.

"I'm not surprised," she said blandly.

"Because you lied to me?"

"Because privacy laws protect people like Márya, Ms. Mendelev, from people like you."

"People like me?"

"People who want access to someone's medical records so they can use the information for personal gain."

He leaned forward. "I have absolutely nothing to gain from this. I'm here on behalf of my stepmother, who only wants what's best for her grandchild, if she has one."

"What's best for the child—or what's best for her? Does she really care about this supposed grandchild, or does she see it as a chance for a do-over on motherhood, since she didn't exactly do a great job the first time around? You'll forgive me if I remain unconvinced it's Márya, or any child she might have had, that interests either you or your stepmother."

It rankled to hear his own worries about his stepmother's

motives echoed by this sanctimonious lady lawyer, but Morgan bypassed an angry reply.

Instead he tried to do as Lillian suggested and play to the woman's friendship with Márya Mendelev. "Do you think your friend would want her child to be shuffled through the foster-care system when it has a grandmother, a wealthy grandmother, who's eager to love it and raise it as her own? Would she want to deny her child the chance to have the best of everything?"

Ms. Walker scowled. Apparently Lillian's wealth didn't impress her.

"You must be aware, even if your stepmother isn't, that the odds a healthy baby will remain in foster care for long are slight these days, given the high demand for adoptable infants."

"Before the child could be adopted, there would have to be a good-faith search for any living relatives. Given Charlie's criminal record, we wouldn't be hard to find."

A flash of some strong emotion crossed Ms. Walker's face before the professional mask dropped back in place.

"Which is one more reason to believe there was no child. Or, if there was, that it might have been claimed by relatives on Ms. Mendelev's side of the family."

Was that who she was protecting? He made a non-committal sound, clicked open his smartphone and scanned the file of emails from the P.I. No, he remembered correctly.

"According to Ms. Mendelev's application for a student visa, she had no living relatives. Her family was wiped out in the civil war in her home country. Unless she lied to the immigration people."

The woman across from him licked her lips, drawing his attention to their soft fullness, reminding him of that fleeting smile. He gave a silent sigh and refocused on the business at hand.

"How did you gain access to that information?"

"The private investigator . . ." had better luck bribing the staff at the college the Mendelev woman had attended than he'd had bribing the staff at the homeless shelters, but Morgan wasn't about to tell the lady lawyer that. " . . . accessed her records online."

"Be that as it may, I'm afraid you'll have to accept the fact that this supposed child was a figment of your P.I.'s imagination."

He leaned in, temper tightly reined. "You said yourself Ms. Mendelev was pregnant when you first met her."

She leaned forward as well, green eyes fixed on his. "Do you want to know how many times your brother had kicked her in the belly before she managed to get away from him?"

He couldn't help but flinch as he settled back in his chair. "You're saying categorically that she was no longer pregnant by the time she arrived in Los Angeles County?"

No hesitation, no shifting of her eyes. "Yes."

So it was over.

He dreaded telling Lillian, but at least he could get back to Boston tomorrow. And Charlie's mother didn't need to know all the unpleasant details.

His eyes slid to the colorful painting over Ms. Walker's head.

Tomorrow was Saturday. Maybe he could stay here over the weekend and do the icy lady lawyer a favor. After all, she had helped the Mendelev woman get away from Charlie and taken her to a hospital, so in a way she'd tried to save Lillian's grandchild.

Now they'd gotten all that behind them, maybe he and Ms. Walker could start over again, without any ulterior motives to interfere with the magnetic hum of attraction he felt for her, an attraction he'd bet his last million she felt as strongly as he did.

Rosalie made a show of gathering up the few scattered papers on her desk, but Mr. Danby didn't take the hint. Instead, he crossed his long legs and gave her a calculating look.

"Have you and your father considered selling your mother's work? You could get several thousand dollars apiece for them."

Obviously a man who put a cash value on everything.

"My father has been out of the picture since before Mother . . . before she started to paint seriously," she told him with as thin a veneer of politeness as she could manage. "And even if I wanted to sell any of her work, I wouldn't know how."

"I might be able to help you. I'm not an art critic, as you put it, but I do have a private collection that has allowed me to develop relationships with several very successful art dealers. I know of one in Beverly Hills who specializes in the kind of paintings your mother did."

"I'm surprised you'd buy anything from someone who deals in, quote, middle-brow art."

"Not my usual taste, but I bought something for a friend who enjoys that sort of thing."

"Why would I want to sell my mother's paintings?" Especially on the recommendation of someone with so little respect for her work. "I don't need the money."

"Of course not. How many of them do you have?"

She thought of the cluttered, sunlit studio at home.

"Dozens, I'd guess."

"Wouldn't your mother want people to enjoy her work, instead of having the paintings stashed away in some spare room?"

With Rosalie's home office crammed into one corner of her bedroom after she'd moved Joey into the smaller bedroom, her mother's studio wasn't exactly a spare room anymore. Rosalie remembered how happy it had always made her mother to give a painting to a friend. She'd spend hours to find the right one for that particular person, and was so happy when she saw any of her work in someone's home. But to sell her paintings . . .

"No, I'm sorry, Mr. Danby."

"Morgan." His smile upgraded from charming to dazzling.

She ignored the slow burn that lit in her belly, the forgotten dreams it rekindled.

"I'm sorry. I'm not prepared to sell them."

"I didn't take you for a selfish woman, Ms. Walker."

He emphasized the last two words in unspoken invitation, but she couldn't invite him to call her Rosalie. Not when his words sent a wave of doubt and shame washing over her.

Was it selfish to keep Joey's existence a secret from his grandmother? Would Márya really want her to go that far? She needed to think about that. She'd already spent the last few nights thinking about nothing else, but now Mr. Danby, Morgan, had given up his search, she needed to be certain, once and for all, that she'd done the right thing.

But this wasn't a good time to rethink things, not while Morgan's thousand-watt smile dazzled her, his navy blue eyes fascinated her, and the musky scent of his expensive cologne filled the air around her. Right now she needed to get the man out of her office.

She shuffled more papers around her desk. "Selfish?"

"If I were you, I'd want to celebrate my mother's talent. Would she have turned down an opportunity like this?"

Rosalie blinked. She hadn't thought of it that way.

He pressed his advantage.

"I'd be glad to take a few of her paintings to my friend's gallery. I'm sure he'd be happy to show them."

"Why would he want to show the work of an amateur painter?"

"Your mother may not have sold any of her work, but she was no amateur. She must have studied art somewhere."

She pushed the flow of pink-tinted memories away. "In college. Then after . . . when she first began to paint again, she took more classes."

"Not at the local community center." It wasn't a question.

"No. UCLA. She was in a couple of student shows up there, but her paintings didn't sell."

"Too conventional for that crowd. But not for the patrons of my friend's gallery. These paintings are exactly what they want to decorate their winter homes in Palm Springs."

The memories swirled into a rainbow-colored dance in Rosalie's head. Her mother would have been so thrilled by an offer like this. And the money could go into Joey's college fund.

"I'm not sure . . ."

"What if I came by your house this evening to look at the other paintings you have? I could pick two or three and show them to my friend tomorrow to see what he has to say."

"No!"

Panic pushed the word out before Rosalie could think, could even breathe. Had he guessed her secret? Was all this talk about the paintings a ploy to get inside her house? What would he do if he found out she'd lied to him?

Then she realized her sharp response and flushed face might make Morgan suspicious.

She forced her voice back to normal. "Tonight isn't convenient."

"What about tomorrow?"

There had to be a way to protect Joey without passing up this chance to honor her mother's memory. Maybe . . .

"I could bring a few paintings to your hotel."

Morgan shook his head. "I'd need to see more than a few. If you aren't familiar with the art market, you might not know which ones would sell well, and this art dealer won't want to waste his time with anything but your mother's most saleable work."

Her mind went into overdrive. She hated to let this incredible opportunity slip by.

She could set up a playdate for Joey. It wouldn't be hard to hide all the toys and other signs he lived there if she kept Morgan out of the back part of the house. She'd just have to display the paintings somewhere other than the studio, which was right next to Joey's bedroom.

She took so long weighing the pros and cons that Morgan shifted impatiently in his chair.

"Would tomorrow around lunchtime work?" she suggested. "Eleven-thirty?"

"That would be fine."

They stood and said goodbye with another hand shake. If this one sizzled through Rosalie's system a little too long, stirred needs and feelings best left unfelt, she ignored it.

As soon as Morgan Danby was out the door, she let out a long breath, sat down and spun her desk chair around in a slow circle of celebration.

He'd given up trying to find Joey. She grinned at the tiny picture stuck on the computer monitor. Her little boy was safe!

When Morgan parked in front of Ms. Walker's Spanish-style bungalow at precisely eleven-thirty the next day, his mouth lifted in an inexplicable smile, although he couldn't have said why. The paintings weren't worth that much money. The finder's fee Morgan had turned down wouldn't have paid for one day's rental on the Porsche.

The unfamiliar need to smile certainly couldn't have anything to do with seeing Ms. Walker again. Any woman who lived in a cozy house like this could only lead him into the kind of emotional morass he'd spent his entire adult life running away from.

The stone path to the house ran between artfully random beds of brightly colored blooms. A patch of tall, pink flowers on bare stems stood by the front door like dainty sentinels, but gave off a sweet perfume that screamed "female territory".

He'd take that as a warning. He knocked on the door, then noticed the doorbell. Before he could decide whether to ring, the door opened.

It took him a full minute to recognize the woman on the other side as Rosalie Walker, lady lawyer. Gone were the dark-colored suits, high-necked knit tops, and sensible black heels.

In their place was a floaty dress covered with flowers that

23

mimicked the display outside, a pair of sandals that displayed bare, oddly appealing toes, and a length of shapely leg.

The only recognizable thing was her wary expression. She'd let her dark-brown hair curl around her face, but pushed it back when she saw him as if uncertain what to do with the hand that wasn't holding the door.

"Hello. Please come in."

In sharp contrast to her sleekly efficient office, Ms. Walker's living room was like something out of a country living magazine. A closer look revealed that the floral curtains and sofa covers had probably been home-made, and not recently. Worn patches marred the soft-brown carpet and the armchair she steered him away from had at least one bad spring.

"Genteel poverty" was the best description of the decor, although owning a house like this free and clear in L.A. ruled literal poverty out of the question. He would have to rethink the sugar-daddy hypothesis, though. For some reason, his mood brightened.

"I'm afraid I don't have all the paintings ready," she told him once he was settled on the sofa. "Can I get you something to drink while you wait? I'll only be a few minutes."

He could imagine what kind of ultra-feminine beverage she might consider appropriate to the occasion. "No, thank you."

She disappeared down the hall that led toward the back of the house, but he wasn't left alone. The two cats he'd seen in the window before, one white with black splotches, the other black on top and white underneath, crept from behind the broken armchair.

The mostly black one jumped on the sofa and sat down next to him, eyes alert, tail twitching. The inner guard, he decided, now he was past the pink sentinels outside.

The mostly white cat jumped up beside him in a more leisurely fashion. It sat very close and put one front paw, then the other, on Morgan's thigh. Daintily it lowered its coal-black nose and sniffed his crotch.

Strangely uncomfortable at the cat's inspection, Morgan managed not to push it away, intrigued with what it might do next. He'd never been allowed to have pets as a kid.

The initial part of the procedure complete, the animal walked its front paws up his polo shirt, claws out enough to gain some purchase, but not enough to scratch. Reaching Morgan's face, it sniffed again, then butted its head against his cheek.

He refused to flinch, or to follow the instinct that made him want to run his hand down the animal's sleek body.

Was the creature purring?

"Smudge!"

The cat turned to give its owner the look of someone doing his duty, then dropped its paws to the sofa cushion and assumed the same position as its comrade.

The pink on Ms. Walker's cheeks when she rushed over made his mind wander to other ways he might make the prim lady lawyer blush.

"I hope you're not allergic. He's never done that before. All I can think of to explain it is that Aaron has a beard, so he's not used to clean-shaven men."

Aaron? And the cat was only familiar with one man? Morgan's mood went sour again.

"Guys." Both cats looked at her. "Off the sofa."

They both jumped down and sauntered away, tails high.

"Smudge and Sylvester. Rescue cats. Brothers. Neutered."

"Where did you set up the paintings?" he interrupted gruffly. "In your mother's studio?"

A shadow flickered in her eyes. "You can only display one or two at a time in there. I picked out a dozen and put them in the dining room."

She led him across the tiled entry to where she'd leaned the larger paintings on the chairs that went with the undistinguished dining table and split the smaller ones between the buffet and sideboard. He could see at once that the prospect of selling dozens of these paintings would make the art dealer's heart pound with avaricious delight.

Rosalie stood in the archway between the entry and dining room while Morgan Danby wandered from painting to painting, occasionally picking one up to hold it to the sunlight.

With an effort, she managed not to fidget with the stress of having this man within yards of Joey's bedroom, despite the fact that Joey himself was safely down the street on his playdate.

At least she wasn't afraid of Mr. Danby, even if he did claim Charlie for a brother. Maybe it was because the change from suit and tie to a blue shirt that accented those killer eyes and jeans that hugged his admirable physique made him look like the proverbial guy next door.

If the guy next door was a movie star. Too bad such an attractive package was wasted on such an arrogant, and for her, dangerous man. When he'd tried to be friendly, to act like the careless charmer he appeared to be, the effect had been pretty devastating.

At the same time, the melancholy she sensed under all the charm made her want to know more about him. He'd tolerated her cats, who tried even Aaron's patience. Mr. Danby seemed to care about his stepmother. And he'd understood how Rosalie felt about her mother's paintings.

Reality jolted her back a step. Being physically attracted to Morgan Danby was bad enough. She didn't dare allow herself to like the man.

Finally he picked out one of the smaller paintings, an iris in vivid purple. "This will be a good sample, and that." He pointed to one of the larger ones, a hillside of poppies and lupins with a single scrub oak to one side. "Do you have any more with children in them?"

She shook her head. "Just the one in my office. My mother gave it to me as a Christmas gift one year. She wasn't interested in people as subjects. She thought it was intrusive to try to show what someone 'really' looked like. She preferred flowers."

"Luckily flowers sell well."

"I'm not doing this for the money."

He nodded absently and handed her the smaller painting. "Would you mind carrying this out to the car for me while I get the larger one?"

For a moment her body quivered with relief that he was leaving. She took the painting and followed him out to the shiny black sports car.

Mrs. Peterson across the street was making a show of raking her already perfectly manicured lawn, eyes fixed on the stranger's expensive car.

"Nice day," she called with a wave.

Rosalie waved back. Once Morgan clicked the car's locks, she opened the door and bent to set the smaller painting on the passenger seat.

"How's Joey?" Mrs. Peterson asked.

Rosalie straightened so quickly out of the car's narrow doorway that she hit her head hard enough to make her ears ring. "He's fine."

Morgan's face twisted for a moment, then went bland and cold.

She didn't dare do anything that might lead to a conversation between him and her neighbor, so she stood there, holding her breath.

Mrs. Peterson gave her a long look. "Well, give Joey a hug for me," before she gave up the pretense of raking and disappeared around the side of her house.

"Joey? I thought his name was Aaron."

Ordinarily the disdain in Morgan's voice would have annoyed Rosalie, but under the circumstances she could have kissed him for his mistake.

Relief slumped one hip against the car. Or maybe it was the idea of kissing Morgan had made her knees so wobbly.

"Mrs. Peterson gets confused," she said.

27

"Humph." He put the larger painting behind the seat, slammed the passenger door shut, and went around to the driver's side.

She stepped away from the car. "Thank you for showing the paintings to your friend."

"I'm an art lover, what can I say?"

His smile made her heart want to burst into sappy, sentimental songs.

This man was the enemy, she reminded herself. Even if he was a spectacularly gorgeous enemy.

"I'll let you know what the dealer says."

She sighed when he drove off, unsure whether it was from relief or longing.

Morgan realized too late it was a mistake to call Lillian from the condo that afternoon before he called Rosalie to report back on his visit to the art dealer.

"You're not giving up?" his stepmother asked plaintively.

"I've run out of leads, and I need to get back to work."

"You believe what that woman told you?"

He thought a moment. "Yes. I'm sure she was telling the truth."

"Men can be so stupid when it comes to a pretty face."

He started to say Rosalie's face wasn't pretty, but it was. Very pretty. Maybe beautiful. When she forgot to be wary and angry.

"If you couldn't get anywhere with the sympathy angle, have you tried the famous Danby charm to get her to tell you where my grandchild is?"

"Lillian, there is no grandchild."

"Without a death certificate, you can't be sure of that."

"But I can't get a death certificate if I don't know the child's name, or when or where it may have died." Or was born.

He sat up straighter in his chair.

Damn. Why hadn't he realized that there could be more than one reason Márya wasn't pregnant when she came to L.A.? The blasted lady lawyer might have tricked him after all.

"Morgan, talk to her one more time."

He would definitely talk to Ms. Walker one more time. The sexy, scheming little . . .

Sexy? How could he still think of the lying lady lawyer as sexy?

"All right, Lillian."

Luckily, the art dealer's enthusiasm for the paintings by Ms. Walker's mother gave Morgan a perfect pretense for seeing her again. He said goodbye to his stepmother and punched in Ms. Walker's number. A few minutes later he disconnected with a smile. An appointment for Monday afternoon was perfect.

The first thing Rosalie noticed when Morgan walked into her office on Monday afternoon was that he didn't have the two paintings with him.

Well, that was the second thing she noticed, after taking in how good he looked in designer black jeans, white shirt, and brown suede jacket. She couldn't stop herself from smiling at him. She gestured him to a chair and sat down, expecting a report on his visit to the art gallery.

Instead she got a sucker punch to the gut.

"How many weeks' pregnant did you say Márya Mendelev was when you first met her?"

"Three months."

He watched her face carefully as she answered, but it was the truth. That was what she'd said. She knew she was a bad liar, so she'd made a mental note of her exact words.

Still, her heart beat a jerky rhythm from the surprise attack she'd barely managed to deflect. What had happened to make him suspicious again?

"And she filed for protection in L.A. three months later?"

Rosalie remained frozen, afraid any move, the slightest change in facial expression, might give her away. "Approximately. I'd have to check the exact date."

"Which means that the child could have been born in the

meantime. A six-month pregnancy isn't all that unusual."

"It's rare enough." She thanked her legal training for the ability to focus on the facts, not the rush of adrenalin speeding through her system. "Rarer than a miscarriage due to a violent attack on the mother. You're clutching at straws, Mr. Danby."

"But if Charlie beat this woman . . ." Rosalie flinched. "If his attack on Ms. Mendelev resulted in the death of an unborn child, why wasn't a police report filed?"

On firmer ground, she took a deep breath. "The assault occurred in Yosemite, on federal land. The death would be reported in the city of Merced. Ms. Mendelev and her attacker lived in rural Merced County. Even if she hadn't been grief-stricken and justifiably frightened to death of Charlie, to whom would she report it? Feds? Police? Sheriff?"

"Wouldn't the hospital report it to the police in Merced?" he asked with a nasty smile.

"They might have if she hadn't lied and told them she fell."

"The hospital believed her injuries were due to a fall?"

"Of course not. But as long as she stuck to that story, they had no option."

He leaned forward, the nasty smile now a nasty glare. "What about you, Ms. Walker? You obviously didn't believe her story. Why didn't you report it to the proper authorities?"

"Márya was too afraid of Charlie."

"Wouldn't she have been safer with Charlie in jail?"

"Until he got out. How much do you know about family violence, Mr. Danby?"

"Too much." His curt answer seemed to surprise even him. "But that's beside the point. As an officer of the court, you had a duty to see the crime was reported."

"Not if the victim and only witness refused to cooperate."

"It was your duty to persuade her to cooperate. You practice family law. You must have dealt with domestic assault before. Why was this case any different from those?"

Rosalie had tried not to say too much about Márya's legal situation, partly to protect her privacy, partly to deprive Morgan Danby of a potential weapon. But now she had no choice.

"I'm surprised your P.I. didn't discover that Ms. Mendelev's immigration status was, shall we say, uncertain. She had a student visa, but your brother persuaded her to leave school. Once she was dependent on him, he told her they'd send her to prison for being an illegal. She was terrified of police and prisons. That's why she stayed with him for as long as she did, and why she didn't file for a protection order until he found her again here in L.A."

Morgan's stomach twisted with disgust. Damn, but Charlie was scum.

He'd been so sure Ms. Walker had lied to him, still wasn't one thousand percent certain she hadn't, but she was a better lawyer than he'd given her credit for. She'd have convinced any jury in the world beyond a reasonable doubt that Márya Mendelev had miscarried after one of Charlie's beatings. If he wasn't convinced, it was because his doubts weren't reasonable. Or because he dreaded telling Lillian.

Ms. Walker's rigid posture showed how much his accusatory tone must have angered her. He wanted to apologize, but wasn't sure how.

Hell, he wanted to do a lot more than apologize. He wanted to bring back the smile she'd greeted him with. He wanted to watch those bare toes wiggle in her sandals.

He was in deep trouble here.

"Are we finished, Mr. Danby?" Rosalie's anger added an extra degree of chill to the words.

"There's still the matter of your mother's paintings."

She'd forgotten about them. "You don't have them with you."

He smiled, but she ignored the illusion of interest in his eyes. He wouldn't fool her again.

31

"They've been sold," he told her.

"What?"

"A woman came into the gallery while I was showing them to my friend, fell in love with them, and insisted on buying them both."

Rosalie ignored the little burst of pleasure at the idea of a total stranger loving her mother's work and leaned back to give him an icy stare.

"Neither you nor your friend were authorized to sell them."

"We explained that to the lady. My friend agreed to hold them for her until you can sign the appropriate contracts."

"What if I don't want to sell them?"

Chapter Three

"Then you're a more spiteful person than I thought," Danby replied. "Why deny this woman the pictures she wants, and yourself the pleasure of sharing your mother's work, because you don't like me?"

He had a point.

"How much did they sell for?" When he told her, she gave a low whistle. Selling even a few paintings at those prices would make a nice addition to Joey's college fund. "I assume you have the contracts with you?"

A few minutes later Rosalie had made Morgan's friend the representative for the sale of her mother's paintings and committed herself to delivering two dozen more to the gallery by the end of the week. Once the paperwork was done, she stood and held out her hand.

"Thank you for helping me find new homes for my mother's work. I hope you have a safe trip back to . . ."

"Boston." He stood too, and took her hand in his.

"Goodbye, Mr. Danby."

He smiled and released her hand slowly. A sensuous tingle crept up her arm.

"It's been a pleasure, Ms. Walker."

She started to say it hadn't, to echo what he'd said when they first met, but she couldn't. How sad was that?

She watched him walk out the door, and out of her life, with a mixture of profound relief and regret. She looked down. The picture of Joey on her computer monitor beamed up at her, reminding her of what really mattered. There were other men, although few with the magnetism of Morgan Danby, but there was only one Joey.

Rosalie took the promised paintings to the gallery the next Saturday, but daily life soon pushed them out of her mind. When an engraved envelope arrived in her office mail three weeks later, she didn't know what it was at first. The return address reminded her. It was an invitation to the opening of her mother's show.

Her heart danced at idea of seeing others celebrate, and love, her mother's work. Then she groaned at the thought of having to get dressed up after a long day at work, drive all the way to Beverly Hills, and try to find a place to park.

After a moment, she realized she couldn't go in any case. The opening was next Thursday. Jill, the teenage neighbor who some-times took care of Joey, wasn't allowed to babysit on school nights. Her parents might have made an exception, but the opening didn't start until eight and, with the drive, it would be past eleven before Rosalie got home.

She put the envelope on her desk and turned back to the rest of her mail.

"What's this?" Vanessa picked up the envelope after she set the sandwich she'd bought for Rosalie on the desk a couple of hours later.

"An invitation to the opening of that show of my mother's paintings I told you about."

"Beverly Hills!" Vanessa sat down and took the invitation out to read it. "Sounds fancy. What are you going to wear?"

"Can't go." Rosalie shrugged at her friend's shocked expression. "No one to watch Joey."

"Rosie, you've got to go. You can't miss your mom's big moment. There must be someone who can watch Joey."

Rosalie shook her head.

"What about that older lady across the street?"

"Mrs. Peterson's in Omaha visiting the grandchildren." Rosalie took a drink of coffee.

Vanessa reread the invitation. "This thing starts at eight. Won't Joey be asleep by then?"

Rosalie almost choked on her coffee. "Asleep or awake, I am *not* leaving him alone!"

"Hey, calm down. I may not be Ms. Maternal here, but I'd never suggest anything like that. Give me some credit. What I was thinking was maybe I could watch him for you."

"You?"

"He'd be asleep."

Rosalie laughed. "Until he wakes up. Then what?"

"If he's hungry I feed him. If he's wet I change him."

"What if he's worse than wet?"

Vanessa grimaced. "I change him anyway?"

"Not exactly a professional babysitter attitude. Besides, you have to argue in front of the Federal Court of Appeals next Friday, don't you? You'll need your sleep the night before, and I may not get back until late."

"True." Vanessa slumped back in the chair, then sat up again with a grin. "Did you know Aaron was the oldest of six?"

"What does the size of your husband's family have to do with anything, other than the decision the two of you have made to remain childless?"

"I'll bet he changed a lot of diapers once upon a time. Maybe it's like riding a bicycle, something you never forget how to do. He and I could both come over. If you're out too late, I can nap on the couch while Aaron takes over with the kid."

"I suspect Aaron will have to change any diapers that need it, even if you're awake."

"Whatever. The point is, now you can go to the opening."

The happiness that flooded Rosalie's heart told her how badly she wanted to be there for her mother's big night.

"If it's okay with Aaron, I guess it's okay with me."

"Great! So . . ." Vanessa leaned forward as if to say something terribly important. "What are you going to wear?"

The day of the opening Joey woke up with a cold. Rosalie rearranged her schedule so she could stay home from the office to take care of him, but she hated to miss the opening of her mother's show.

When she called Vanessa to cancel, her friend insisted she could still babysit Joey. "If he's asleep, it won't matter, will it?"

"Yes, but there's still the little matter of what happens if he wakes up."

"Aaron can handle it. When I asked him about coming with me to watch Joey, he let it drop that one of the jobs he once had between acting gigs was as a nanny. He's a pro with kids."

Rosalie couldn't quite picture Vanessa's Aaron, six feet tall and two hundred pounds of solid muscle, as a nanny, but the man had a heart as big as he was, so maybe it would be okay.

"Rosie, you know you want to do this. You have to do this."

Vanessa was right.

"Okay. I'll see you at seven-thirty."

"We'll be there. You don't have to worry about a thing."

Morgan walked into the crowded art gallery and realized he was in more trouble than he'd thought.

He hadn't asked himself why he'd shown up here tonight. He was back in L.A. on business, so it had seemed reasonable to see how the paintings by Ms. Walker's mother sold.

He should have known better. As soon as he saw Rosalie on

the other side of the room in a high-necked, knee-length black dress that showed off all her curves, a hot flash of need jolted through him. Almost against his will, his eyes tracked down her shapely legs to high-heeled black sandals and those delightful toes. Since when had he ever found toes sexy?

Since when had he ever found lady lawyers sexy?

A waiter wandered by with a tray of drinks. Morgan sighed at the white wine in plastic glasses. Probably Chardonnay, and cheap Chardonnay at that. Still, better than nothing.

He took a glass and sipped it warily. He grimaced at the raw edge of the wine, but his eyes remained fixed on the unfamiliar sight of Rosalie Walker looking happy.

She wasn't totally relaxed. A thin line between her eyebrows showed the stress of being the center of attention in a room full of strangers, but she was smiling as she chatted with an older woman in a designer gown with huge diamonds at her neck and wrist. While the smile faded after the woman walked away, Rosalie still glowed with pleasure as she surveyed the crowd that oohed and aahed over her mother's creations.

He wanted to claim her happiness as his doing, but all he'd done was help her mother find the public she deserved, if too late for her to enjoy it in person.

Still, it looked as if Ms. Walker was enjoying it enough for both of them.

No. He could not continue to think of her as Ms. Walker when every unguarded moment brought new visions of the two of them doing impossibly erotic things with each other.

He took another glass of wine off a passing tray and wandered in her direction, but forced himself to pause and look at the paintings as he went.

His body tightened at the surprised delight in Rosalie's eyes when she saw him, but she quickly turned away. By the time he reached her, the wary look was back.

"Why are you here?" It sounded like an accusation.

He shrugged, vaguely angry at her for being wary, and at himself for apparently bursting the bubble of her happiness.

"My friend sent me an invitation. I was in L.A., so I decided to drop by."

"Why? You've seen my mother's paintings before and, if I remember correctly, didn't think much of them."

"All I said was that they were middle brow art." He took a sip of the wine. "Middle-brow art has its place."

"But not in your collection."

"No, not in mine, but Lillian is quite fond of it. I thought I might find her a birthday gift."

Something in Rosalie's face shifted at Lillian's name.

"I hope you're successful," she said abruptly and walked away.

He started to go after her and explain who Lillian was, but realized it wouldn't help him to remind Rosalie of the whole mess with Charlie.

And, of course, there was Rosalie's bearded Aaron to take into consideration.

So, Morgan let her go. All the same, his eyes continued to drift in her direction as he wandered through the gallery, the way a compass would drift to true north on a sea-tossed sloop.

Rosalie couldn't help but be aware of Morgan Danby watching her.

After all, she had to make a conscious effort not to watch him, an effort that became more of a challenge as the evening progressed. Even when she wasn't looking in his direction, she could feel his eyes on her body, sending an erotic sizzle along her nerves.

Too much wine? Too much celibacy? Too much Morgan Danby.

She was wondering if she could leave yet when she remembered. Lillian was Charlie's mother. Morgan wanted a painting for his stepmother, not a wife, fiancée, or lover. That didn't prove

38

the man was unattached, but the evening seemed younger and her jubilant mood returned.

She decided she owed him an apology for her earlier rudeness. If he was still here.

He was. Standing by himself in front of at a small painting of a single orchid in a sensual shade of pinkish purple. An experiment of her mother's Rosalie had never cared for because its overt sensuality was so out of character, but it had sold for twice as much as the companion painting of a brilliant orange day lily. She scanned the room in hopes he'd move on to something else, but he seemed fascinated by that one painting. When he finally turned away, his eyes went directly to hers. Her heart stumbled at the quirk of a smile he gave her, and her face went hot.

As if on cue, they walked toward each other and met in the middle of the room.

She'd never been good at apologies, but "I'm sorry I walked off like that" came easily, as did the smile she hadn't planned on. Maybe because he smiled back at her in a way that made the tiny pulse at the base of her throat beat double time.

"No problem, Ros—, er, Ms. Walker. You've been under a lot of stress, I'm sure, with all these rich and famous strangers staring at something as personal as your mother's paintings."

Disarmed by his empathy, and by the way her body zipped to attention at the sound of his voice and the smell of his cologne, she looked down at the empty glass in her hand and nodded.

A long moment passed. She cursed herself silently for falling back into the shy little girl she usually kept hidden behind the lawyerly façade, but she still couldn't find anything to say.

When it became clear she wasn't going to hold up her end of the conversation, he asked, "Have you had dinner, Ms. Walker?"

"Rosalie." She was rewarded by a smile that sent butterflies right to her core. "And, yes, we . . . I ate before I left home."

A momentary frown creased his forehead before he said, "Well,

I haven't eaten. Would you like some dessert and a cup of coffee while I have a quick meal?"

The gallery was emptying out. A bored waiter wandered by and offered them the last of the wine in the bottle he held. She shook her head. She'd had enough already. Maybe more than enough, because coffee and something to eat before she drove home sounded like a good idea.

Except, the invitation had come from Morgan Danby. She should say no. He could take everything that mattered away from her.

But he didn't know that. He wanted to give her something.

What harm could there be in taking another hour to cherish the evening's celebration of her mother's work? To learn more about this man before he walked out of her life. An hour she could remember and smile to herself about when she was back in her real world.

"Sure. Where were you thinking about going?"

He grinned and something twisted deep inside her. "Trust me."

The expensive sports car the valet brought around when they stepped out of the gallery was bright red this time. The young man gave it a longing look as he handed Morgan the keys.

"I have to work tomorrow, so we can't go far," Rosalie cautioned in a wistful voice.

"Oh. I was thinking of a place out on the beach near Malibu. We could walk along the sand afterwards, and . . ."

"No," she said with real regret as she climbed into the low-slung car.

By the time he was seated beside her, his grin was back, but he didn't say anything.

He'd driven around the same block twice in search of a parking place before she realized where he was taking her.

"An all-night deli?" Why would a man with Morgan's money eat at a deli, albeit a world-famous one?

"Why not? Incredible cheesecake for you, better pastrami for me than any place I've found in Boston."

Why not? The words buzzed through her mind. Why not let all her responsibilities go, for once, and simply enjoy?

Even if it was the wine that made spending more time with Morgan Danby so appealing, that was only more evidence that she needed time to sober up a bit more before she drove home.

She'd worried about going to a deli dressed up the way she was, but she shouldn't have. Half the women wore dresses fancier than hers, or designer slacks and tops that probably cost ten times as much as her off-the-rack-on-sale best black dress.

The cheesecake was perfect. And after an awkward moment or two, the conversation flowed from topic to topic, light and amusing, although afterwards she couldn't remember exactly what they talked about.

What she did remember was how happy it made her just to be with Morgan, to have him smile at her as if they shared some wonderful secret. Not that they agreed on everything they talked about, but even arguing playfully with him was a joy.

The mood shifted as they lingered over a last cup of espresso.

"Tell me about your mother," Morgan said.

Rosalie closed her eyes and smiled. "She was a free spirit. She loved flowers."

"No surprise there." He chuckled.

"And she loved me." That love had been Rosalie's rock through everything that happened, but the simple words brought a dark shadow to Morgan's face.

"Did she look like you?"

"She was tall, slender, fair. I look more like the women on my father's side of the family."

Morgan's voice was gentle as he asked, "When did he die?"

She stared at the dark liquid in her cup. "He didn't. The day the wheelchair arrived, he left."

Morgan tensed, then let out a long breath. "How long was your mother ill?"

"About fifteen years. That's pretty average for the progressive form of MS she had."

"It must have been hard."

Rosalie shrugged. "We got by. I had to live at home while I was in college and law school, but she made sure my studies came first. We managed pretty well, until . . ." She cleared the tears from her throat. "Until we didn't. I hated it when she had to move to a care facility. She loved her flower garden so much. But she made the best of it. She made the best of everything."

Her tone must have told him she didn't want to go any further down that road, because he let a long silence fall.

As they'd talked, their bodies had shifted until they sat so close together their shoulders touched. Rosalie didn't quite know when during their conversation Morgan had put his hand on her knee, perhaps to emphasize a point he was making, but the weight and warmth of it felt right, as if it belonged there. Being with him, sharing her memories with him, felt right, as if she belonged there.

Then he turned more toward her and the hand moved a few inches up her leg. Closeness became intimacy, warmth became heat, heat became need. Her face almost touching his, she became aware that they were alone in their corner of the dining room.

Something inside her melted. It had been so long since she'd allowed a man to hold her, kiss her . . . Her hands flowed of their own accord to his shoulders and her mind emptied of everything except the hope that he wanted to kiss her as much as she wanted to kiss him.

Morgan was mesmerized by the woman beside him and the sad story she'd told. This woman might understand the sadness that haunted him. More, she had the heart to care about that sadness.

42

He looked into her eyes, surprised to discover the little specks of brown were gone, leaving a pure sea-green a man could drown in.

Her lips were wet and full, as if he'd already kissed them, nipped them, plundered them, as his body had been screaming at him to do since he first saw her in the gallery.

He thought about suggesting they go to the condo, or at least move to the relative privacy of his car, but the moment was too fragile, too precious.

He put both arms around her and drew her closer. His body hardened when his wrist brushed the side of her lush breast. The brief contact made her frown. He charmed the frown away by brushing his lips across her forehead.

When he lowered his head, she lifted her face so he could see her unspoken longing.

The first few bars of "*Für Elise*" broke through the haze of desire. He closed his eyes against the interruption, but managed a smile as he pulled away.

"Your purse is playing music."

Rosalie had been so lost in Morgan's midnight-blue eyes she hadn't heard her cell.

She shook her head to clear it, then gasped and grabbed the phone out of her evening bag, her heart pounding. Joey!

"Yes?" Her voice was a squeak of alarm.

"Rosie, it's the kid." Vanessa sounded half-panicked, too. "He's got a fever of 104 and it's still climbing. At first, he wouldn't stop crying, but now all he does is lie in his crib and whimper. Aaron says it's not serious enough for the emergency room, but he thinks it might be a good idea to take him to the urgent care clinic. What do you think?"

Rosalie forced herself to breathe. She should never have left Joey when he was sick. But guilt—or panic—wasn't what he needed now.

43

"I don't know! Just let me get home. I'll be there as soon as I can."

"Okay. But hurry." Vanessa's voice shook with alarm.

"I will. I promise."

Rosalie clicked off and closed her eyes against the nightmare. She dug around in her purse for the keys. To a car that was parked half-way across Beverly Hills.

"What's wrong?" Morgan asked, his face a polite mask.

"Can you take me back to my car? I need to get home right away because . . ."

She couldn't tell him why. Despite how much she'd enjoyed her time with him, he was still the enemy. She should never have let herself forget that.

"Because something's happened," she told him. "I have to get home."

"Okay."

His tone sounded wrong, but she didn't have time now to figure out why. She had to get home to Joey.

Morgan threw some bills on the table to cover their tab and followed her as she rushed out of the deli. "Where are you parked?"

When she told him, he said, "You can leave your car there overnight. I'll take you home."

"No. Please, just take me to my car."

He opened the car door for her and she slid in.

"You'll get home much faster if you let me drive you straight home."

Her mind was too numb with fear to be able to choose between the time letting Morgan drive would save and the risk of having him anywhere near Joey. When Morgan turned his car toward the freeway, she didn't protest.

With the light late night traffic and a heavier-than-legal foot on the gas, he had her home in fifteen minutes, but by the time he drove up in front of the house her chest was so tight she could barely breathe, much less think. She bolted out of the car as soon as it stopped and dashed up the walk.

Aaron had seen her coming and held the front door open, the front-hall light a beacon, and shut it behind her as she ran in.

Morgan sat in the dark car, unsure what had happened. Or rather, unsure of what it meant.

One minute he'd been half intoxicated with touching Rosalie, fascinated with the promise, even eagerness in her eyes. The next minute it was as if he'd stepped into a different reality.

With her so close, he'd forgotten about everything that might stand between them, about Lillian and Charlie, about Aaron. Maybe Aaron was where he'd gone wrong.

Rosalie had been in a state of panic the moment her cell rang. By the time they got to her house, she'd seemed scared to death. Morgan had thought maybe her Aaron was sick or injured, but, no, he'd been waiting for her at the door when they got there, a dark shadow twice her size.

Could there be a more sinister reason for her intense feelings about Charlie and the woman he'd murdered? Was that why the usually cool Ms. Walker had been so nervous the day he was at the house? Why she'd jumped so much when the neighborhood busybody mentioned Joey/Aaron's name that she'd nearly given herself a concussion?

Morgan drove away, a sick dread in his stomach.

He slept in fits and spurts, and got up the next morning feeling as if something dark and dangerous was closing in on him.

When coffee and breakfast did nothing to ease his mood, he had his assistant in Boston reschedule his flight home before he called Rosalie's office.

"I'm sorry," the male receptionist intoned in his out-of-work actor's baritone, "Ms. Walker isn't in. She won't be again until Monday."

Anger shot through Morgan's system. Had that big jerk beaten Rosalie up last night?

He thanked the receptionist and headed for the car. He needed to get to her house and make sure she was okay.

Joey's wail broke through the black haze of exhaustion and pulled Rosalie out of her bed.

When she reach his room, tears flowed down her cheeks at the sight of him standing there rocking side to side while clutching the side of his crib, the way he did every morning.

A quick touch to his cheek told her the fever was still down. The medicine they'd given him at the urgent care center had done the trick. She lifted him from the crib and gave him a ferocious hug.

"Okay, food or diaper first?"

"Best."

"Breakfast it is. I bet you're hungry. Vanessa said you didn't want your bedtime bottle," she murmured as she put him down and took his tiny hand in hers so he could toddle beside her to the kitchen. "You gave her and Aaron a real scare last night, you know."

"Vessa," Joey echoed. "Run."

She lifted him into his highchair, mixed his cereal and set it in the microwave.

"Yes, Vanessa and Aaron watched you last night."

The sudden memory of what she'd been doing while they'd dealt with Joey's fever froze her in place until the microwave's penetrating ding brought her back to the moment.

She'd almost been kissed by Morgan Danby. Had almost kissed him back.

The man who claimed Charlie Thompson for his brother. The man who could take Joey away from her.

Shame washed over her.

Joey made an impatient sound. She finished fixing his cereal

46

and set it on the highchair. With luck he wouldn't demand that she feed him. She needed time to pull herself together.

Automatically she fed the cats, who were twining around her legs. When the coffee-maker sputtered to a stop she poured herself a cup and stood by the sink to drink the bitter liquid.

Instead of pulling herself together, she fell apart more. Márya's will gave her custody of Joey, but that wasn't the final word. Not in the face of blood relatives, wealthy blood relatives who wanted him. And the fact that she'd deceived those relatives would count against her in court. But what else could she have done?

The questions and the guilt, spun deeper and deeper. But one thing was clear. She must never get within kissing distance of Morgan Danby again.

A clatter and plop on the floor told her Joey had had enough breakfast. She took a deep breath before she bent down to right the bowl and wipe the cereal off the floor.

By the time they were both dressed, Joey was restless. Maybe she could drive him out to a playground at the beach.

That's when she remembered her car was still in Beverly Hills.

If she'd been thinking more clearly last night she wouldn't have this problem. But letting Morgan Danby take the weight of making even one decision off her shoulders had been too tempting. Everything about him had been too tempting.

She didn't let herself think about what it would be like to have someone around to help her make decisions all the time, someone to share the burdens and joys of raising Joey.

"Pak." Joey bounced in his playpen. "Pak!"

"Okay, tiger. We'll go to our usual park. Let me get a jacket from your closet."

In his room she noticed a bag of his outgrown clothes that she'd set aside to pass along to a neighbor down the street who had a boy two months younger than Joey. Maybe she could borrow their car seat and take an expensive taxi ride to Beverly Hills to pick up her car.

She bundled Joey up, put on her own jacket, and picked him up for the short walk down to the neighbor's.

"So, Joey . . ." she started as she opened the front door.

Morgan Danby stood on the other side, one hand raised to knock.

Chapter Four

Rosalie's heart stuttered, stopped, raced. It took every ounce of energy she had to breathe. Tense, painful seconds ticked by while the three of them silently stared at each other.

"No!" Joey cried suddenly, pointing down.

Smudge was trying to slip past her legs out the open door. Sylvester, as usual, was right on his heels.

Morgan crouched down to block the cats' path, then raised his head, eyes boring through her. "Why don't we all go inside?"

She nodded numbly as she stepped away and let him herd the cats back into the house. He shut the door with a noise that was only fractions short of a slam.

"The living room?" he suggested, when she still couldn't find any words or the breath to say them.

He looked around the room at the playpen and scattering of toys she'd hidden away so carefully when he'd been there before. Joey squirmed and kicked to get down, but she held him tighter, stroking his head to calm him. Fear, anger, regret burned her throat to silence.

Morgan turned his attention to the child in her arms.

"Joey?"

The boy giggled at his own name, then buried his head in her shoulder.

"Josef, perhaps? For Ms. Mendelev's father?"

She made the mistake of looking Morgan in the eye. The rage that glowed there stifled any possible defense she might have thought she could offer.

He laughed, a mixture of anger and triumph that sent an arctic chill down her spine and made her hold the precious bundle in her arms so close Joey gave a squeak of protest.

"It's all in my favor, isn't it," Morgan went on. "Or Lillian's favor. Trying to keep the child secret from her won't serve you well in court. Of course, you know that."

The words shattered the icy fear that held her silent and immobile. Finally able to draw a full breath, she set Joey in his playpen and blindly handed him his favorite stuffed bear.

"I also know the woman who raised Charlie Thompson should never be allowed to raise another child."

"She raised me, too."

That stopped her for a half a beat. "I rest my case."

The last remnants of polite charm vanished from his face.

"You'll hear from my stepmother's lawyer soon, Ms. Walker. Very soon."

Before she caught her breath, he was gone.

"Bye-bye," Joey said solemnly.

Morgan drove the rented Ferrari to the nearest commercial street and pulled into the parking lot of one of L.A.'s ubiquitous strip malls.

He needed to let the rage boil off so he could think. He never acted out of anger. He wasn't that kind of man. He wasn't like Charlie.

The image of a small face framed by red-blonde curls floated into his mind. Damn if Joey didn't look like the pictures Lillian had of Charlie as a baby, or a toddler, or whatever you called a kid that age.

Morgan took another deep breath and wished it was late enough in the day to have a drink. No, he didn't. He wasn't that kind of man, either.

So, what to do now? How could be get some payback at the sneaky Ms. Walker for what she'd put him through?

She hadn't lied to him in her capacity as an attorney, so disbarment wasn't an issue. His friend's gallery had already sold most of her mother's paintings, so he couldn't stop that from happening. Not that Ms. Walker cared about the money.

Then, the obvious answer. Nothing would hurt her more than taking away the kid she'd clung to for dear life during most of their brief conversation. She clearly loved the little bastard. Love always made it easy for people to hurt you.

Despite the threats he'd made, he'd never really intended to help Lillian get custody if the kid already had a decent home. He'd hoped she'd settle for visitation rights. Rights she'd probably never use, since it would mean disrupting her life in Boston to travel to Los Angeles. His main goal had been to keep Charlie's father from getting at the kid.

Ms. Walker's lies changed everything.

Not only did they give him a good reason to carry out the charge Lillian had given him to bring Charlie's child home, they also made it easier for him to do that. He could make Lillian happy and have his revenge on the lady lawyer, too.

As his anger faded, cold reason raised its ugly head. If given the choice, wouldn't Rosalie rather have him hurt her physically than take kid away from her?

He shook off the uncomfortable implications of that thought and looked out at the string of fast-food restaurants in front of him.

Two boys walked along the sidewalk. Suddenly the larger one lunged sideways and pushed the smaller off the curb and into the parking lot. The harried-looking woman a few feet ahead of them turned at something the larger one said, then yelled a curse at the smaller one and grabbed his arm to yank him back up on the curb, oblivious to the larger one's smirk.

Something twisted inside of Morgan. The hopeless expression on the younger boy's face reminded him too starkly of his own past.

And of the look in Rosalie's eyes when he'd stormed out of her house.

Sure, the lovely Ms. Walker had tricked him. But maybe revenge wasn't the best reason for whatever he did next. Maybe he should be thinking about what was best for Charlie's kid.

Rosalie was lucky enough to get an appointment with Joey's social worker on Monday morning. Ms. Cameron was so overloaded with cases she often took as long as a week to return a phone call, but someone had cancelled and Rosalie managed to get the free spot.

"I'm so glad you've finally decided to go through with the adoption," Ms. Cameron told her. "You and Joey both need the closure."

The social worker's cheerful smile grated against nerves worn raw by worry and guilt.

Rosalie cleared her throat and managed to say, "Yes," in an almost-normal voice.

Ms. Cameron glanced over the forms Rosalie had spent some of the sleepless hours of the last three nights completing. When the social worker got to the last page, she frowned.

"There's a name listed here under next-of-kin, but no contact information. I thought you didn't know whether Joey had any living relatives besides his father or not."

"I didn't." Rosalie swallowed. "His father's mother contacted me recently."

Ms. Cameron set the sheaf of papers down. "What's she like?"

Rosalie closed her eyes against the image of Morgan Danby's face that danced through her mind. "She didn't contact me in person. I met with her stepson."

Ms. Cameron leaned back. "What's he like?"

A litany of inappropriate responses roared through Rosalie's mind. Handsome. Charming. Intelligent. Sexy. Hot. Cold. Angry. And out for revenge.

"Not much like Joey's father, thank goodness. They're very wealthy, apparently."

"Does this grandmother want visitation rights?"

Rosalie swallowed a wave of panic. "I think she may be interested in custody of Joey."

Ms. Cameron raised her eyebrows. "Since you're an attorney, I assume you know what your rights are here."

Rosalie nodded. She'd spent the rest of her sleepless weekend nights making herself an expert on California adoption law.

"Then we'll want to move forward as quickly as possible on the adoption." Ms. Cameron's tone conveyed the optimism Rosalie needed. "First, we'll need to do a DNA test."

"A what?"

"A DNA test to establish that this," she looked down at the papers in front of her, "Lillian Danby is, in fact, Joey's grandmother."

The idea that Márya could have ever cheated on Charlie had never crossed Rosalie's mind. Her friend wouldn't have dared do that, of course, even if she'd been the kind of woman who might have, but for the first time since she'd opened the door to Morgan Danby on Friday morning, Rosalie felt a glimmer of hope.

"How is that done?" she asked. "Would Mrs. Danby have to come to L.A. for the test?"

"No."

Rosalie's hope faded again as Ms. Cameron explained the procedure for DNA tests of this sort. Nothing there to keep Charlie's mother from proving she had a claim to Joey.

"How are my chances?" Rosalie couldn't stop from asking before she left.

"I'd say they're excellent. You're a great mom and Joey loves you. I'll be sure to put that in my report. And you're the guardian his mother chose for him. As long as there's nothing negative in your file, there shouldn't be any problem with the adoption going through."

Nothing negative in the file, such as lying about Joey's existence to his presumably loving and grieving grandmother. Throat too thick with tears for words, Rosalie nodded.

"Give your boy a big kiss for me."

She nodded again and went out to her car, the California sunshine dimmed by her own personal bank of dark clouds.

She'd been a fool. Morgan Danby had taken her by surprise and she'd acted like an idiot.

Not just on Friday, when she'd added insult to injury, but the first time he showed up in her office. She should never have lied to him. She'd known it all along. But the thought of losing Joey had made her stupid. And stupidity never paid.

She drove to her office and grimly dove into the pile of work that waited on her desk.

Lillian was overjoyed, of course. Morgan had decided against telling her on the phone. Instead he waited until he was back in Boston and told her the news over drinks in the conservatory of the Back Bay mansion his family had owed for over a hundred years. The air was thick with the smell of growing things, marred by Lillian's expensive perfume.

"A boy!" His stepmother set down her martini. "Does he look at all like Charlie?"

"Pretty much. He's blonder, I guess."

Lillian smiled coyly and touched her own blonde curls, as if they both didn't know how much she paid every month to keep it that color. "I can hardly wait to see him. How soon can you bring the little angel to me?"

Little imp would be more like it, Morgan suspected.

"You know it's more complicated than that, Lillian. Ms. Walker

54

is the child's legal guardian. You'd have to go to court and get custody of him first."

"Ms. Walker? Isn't she the one who lied to you about whether the child existed? I knew you were letting the woman put one over on you. Men!" She shook her head.

Morgan took a sip of his single malt and forced the image of Rosalie's face out of his mind.

"She misled me, but the boy's mother chose Ms. Walker to be his guardian, and the court is going to give a lot of weight to that, especially given the circumstances of his mother's death."

At least Lillian had the good grace to look uncomfortable. She picked up the martini glass and twisted it in her hand without taking a drink, then set it down again.

"What do I have to do to get my grandson?"

Morgan sighed. "The first step is a DNA test to prove Charlie was his father."

"Do you mean that foreign woman Charlie lived with was sleeping with other men?"

"Of course not. But the court isn't going to take your word for it that you're the child's next-of-kin. They'll want proof."

"Then what?"

Morgan launched into the details of the procedures that he'd studied online before he left California.

"It seems like a great deal of trouble to get my grandson back. After all, he's my own flesh and blood," she protested when he was finished.

"The courts will want what's best for the child."

Lillian gestured broadly to the subtle opulence around them. "I can buy him anything he wants, send him to exclusive schools. How could that not be what's best for him?"

Morgan acted as if it was a rhetorical question and took another sip of his drink.

"You're sure my grandson is okay?" Lillian frowned. "Mentally, I mean?"

"Yes. He seems bright and healthy."

"He wasn't damaged by how that woman lived? Homeless shelters." She shuddered.

"Shelters for battered women," he corrected.

"Whatever." She thought for a minute. "Do you think the court will let me change his name once I have custody? Josef Mendelev sounds so . . . so foreign."

"What would you change it to?"

"I was thinking Charleston Danby would be appropriate."

"You want to name him after Charlie?" Morgan carefully set his glass down to hide the tremor of anger in his hands.

She sat straighter. "Charleston is an old family name. My grandfather was a Charleston."

"Lillian, the boy is almost a year and a half old. Maybe you could change his last name, but he knows his name is Joey. If you don't like Josef, you could change it to Joseph."

Since she pronounced the two names the same way, she gave him a puzzled look in reply.

"Or," he said as casually as he could, "you could leave him with the only mother he remembers. You could visit him every few months, maybe have him come here to visit you during the summer when he's older."

"But she tried to keep my grandson a secret from me. Why would I allow a woman like that to raise him?"

"Because she loves him, and he loves her."

"He'll love me, too, once he knows I'm his grandmother. I don't understand why you'd suggest giving away Charlie's child."

"If you let Ms. Walker have custody, you're likely to get visitation rights. But if you take her to court and she convinces the judge that you're too, um, senior to chase after an active toddler, you might end up with nothing."

She sniffed. "I can hire people to chase after him. That's how I raised you and Charlie."

Which was the whole point, but this wasn't the time for hard truths. "I'm not sure that's what a judge will want to hear."

Harkins, the butler, appeared to announce, in the fake English accent that always grated on Morgan's nerves, that dinner was ready.

"Felicity Mason called this morning and wanted to join us for dinner," Lillian announced as Morgan helped her into her chair at one end of the table that could have seated twelve. "I told her I wanted you to myself this evening."

He gave a low sigh. He wouldn't have minded the distraction of his friend's wry wit.

"I didn't know she was back from France."

He took his usual seat to Lillian's right.

"She came back yesterday. Her mother is delighted to have her home again."

The thoughtful expression on Lillian's face as she took a sip of the soup the maid set in front of her should have been a warning.

"What if you were the one who sued for the custody of Charlie's son?" she asked.

"Me? Why would a judge be any more likely to give me custody than you?"

"Not you—you and Felicity." She gave him a smug look and took another sip of soup. "You've always been friends, and she needs a husband."

He swallowed a laugh. Felicity wasn't in the market for a husband. Never would be. But she kept that part of her life secret from her mother, and her mother's friends.

"Can you picture Felicity chasing around after a child?" he asked.

"No, but you're rich enough to hire someone to chase after him for her, just the way I would. That way I could see my grandson whenever I want."

Which wouldn't be very often, Morgan suspected, once she was reminded of what small children were like.

"Why would Felicity go along with such a crazy plan?"

"You're handsome, rich, and have quite a reputation as a ladies' man, if you know what I mean. Her mother is one of my best friends. Who could be more suitable for Felicity to marry?"

"Someone she loved?" Morgan ventured.

"Love and marriage are two different things."

"You didn't love my father?"

Lillian gave an artful sniff.

"Of course I did. But it also made good practical sense for me and your father to get married and put a stop to all the gossip about our divorces. And it makes good practical sense for you and Felicity to get married now so I can be near my grandchild."

Morgan shook his head. He shouldn't have mentioned Lillian's relationship with his father, but her attitude still rankled.

And continued to rankle throughout dinner as she recited all the advantages, mainly for her, if he married Felicity and adopted Charlie's kid.

Finally he'd had enough. "If you'll excuse me, I'm going to have to skip dessert. I've got a huge backlog of work."

"Can't you stay a little longer? We could talk about your wedding."

He closed his eyes and counted to ten. "There is not going to be a wedding. I am not marrying Felicity to get custody of Charlie's son. Is that clear?"

"You could stay and tell me more about my grandson."

"I only saw him for a few minutes, so I don't know much. He's a cute kid. He's learning to talk. He loves his mother."

"She's not his mother, and she's never going to be. I'm his grandmother, so I have some say in who raises the poor child. He'd learn to love Felicity, too, I'm sure."

Anger pushed him to his feet.

"That's not going to happen, Lillian. And I'd like to keep Felicity as a friend, so I don't want you to even mention your crazy idea to her—or her mother. Got that?"

Lillian heaved a dramatic sigh. "Well, if you're determined to be selfish . . ."

"I'm determined to do what's best for Charlie's son." He bent and dutifully kissed the suspiciously taunt skin of her proffered cheek. "Goodbye, Lillian."

On the drive back to his penthouse condo near the Common, his stepmother's voice echoed in his head. He wanted to do what was best for Joey, but neither Lillian nor Felicity was the answer. And Charlie's father definitely wasn't the answer. Which left Ms. Rosalie Walker.

Morgan shook the thought from his mind and refocused on the work he had to do tonight.

The next Saturday morning, Rosalie opened the front door, Joey on her hip, expecting the babysitter. When she found Morgan on her porch instead, an inexplicable bolt of joy left her speechless.

Her soaring heart had an immediate nosedive. Had he come to take Joey away? The lawyer in her knew he couldn't do that, but the mother in her still went cold.

Luckily, she recovered her sanity before he could worm his way into her house the way he had the last time.

"Why are you here? I'm expecting an important business call and . . ."

As if on cue, the cell in her jeans pocket chimed Beethoven. She groaned and set Joey on the tiled floor of the entry hall. Without taking her eyes off their unexpected visitor, she opened her phone.

"Good morning, Congresswoman Barnes. Thank you for taking the time to talk to me on the weekend. Could you hold for a moment, please?"

She clicked the mute button and looked wildly around for Joey, who had waddled off toward the kitchen. Where was Jill? The teenager had promised to watch him while Rosalie took the business call.

Rosalie chased Joey down and dumped him in his playpen. By the time he was safely corralled, Morgan stood inside the front door, both cats weaving around his legs.

She was stuck. Her client's whole future rested on this phone call. She pushed open one of the living-room windows and waved an arm at Morgan.

"You, out."

When he didn't move, she marched up to him, put her hand on his chest, pushed him back out the front door.

"You, in," she told the cats when they tried to follow him.

Then she came out on the porch, too, and shut the door. As she pulled the cell out of her pocket, she positioned herself so her body blocked the door and she had a clear view of where Joey sat in his playpen chewing on his favorite teddy bear's already-battered ear. With luck, Morgan would get the message and leave.

"Hello, Congresswoman," she said again. "Sorry for the delay. About that private immigration bill for my client . . ."

Morgan tuned out the obviously confidential conversation and scowled down at Rosalie, almost unrecognizable in a sleeveless t-shirt and jeans, her hair haphazardly pulled back.

If she thought he'd leave because she had an important phone call, she had another think coming. He had to do what he'd come here to do and get back to Boston this evening so he could put in a full day at the office tomorrow.

A muted thump drew his attention to the window. The stuffed bear the kid had been holding a moment before was now on the floor a couple of feet from the playpen.

Thump! Bump! A red-and-blue rubber ball followed, bounced twice and landed on the sofa. Then came a square book with thick pages and brightly colored drawings. Thump!

He made the mistake of making eye-contact with the kid, who opened his mouth and began to howl.

Rosalie threw Morgan a harsh glance, then looked past him to the crying child inside. Her frown deepened.

"I'm sorry, Congresswoman. I was distracted for a moment. Could you say that again, please?"

Even a moment of Rosalie's attention had ramped the kid's protest up another notch. Tears ran down his face, which was turning from red to purple.

Rosalie waved her hand at the screaming child, but that only made things worse. The boy's cries began to irritate, plucking every auditory nerve, until Morgan thought his head might explode.

Rosalie gave every sign of being as distressed by the child's crying as he was, but from her frown and the few words he'd caught of the conversation, she was explaining something to the Congresswoman that was of vital importance to Rosalie's client.

He couldn't stand it any longer. He gently took her by both arms and moved her out of the way, ignoring the sizzle her bare skin sent through his system.

The panicky expression on her face made him wonder if she thought he would steal the kid right from under her nose. He shook his head and flung one hand toward the screaming child.

Her body sagged. She didn't try to stop him, but when he walked inside she moved nearer to the window so she could keep a close eye on things.

"An unusual and very deserving case, yes, Congresswoman," she said into the cell.

As soon as Morgan stepped down from the foyer into the living room, the kid stopped crying. He sniffled once and looked up at Morgan.

He and Charlie's son stared each other. The kid wore pull-up jeans, tiny sneakers, and a white t-shirt with little blue soccer balls on it.

Morgan braced himself for another explosion, but the boy held up his arms. "Out."

Morgan shook his head.

"I don't think that would be a wise move. You're more familiar with the layout of this place than I am, and amazingly fast on those little legs of yours."

The kid blinked twice and repeated, "Out."

Time for another tactic. "No."

That got the message through. The kid frowned, gave a little bounce, and said in a louder voice, "Out."

"No."

Morgan sat down on the sofa. Might as well be comfortable while the impending disaster ran its course.

But the kid shifted tactics, too. He reached both hands toward Morgan. "Up?"

Except for his tear-stained face, the boy seemed clean enough, but Morgan sensed a sticky veneer. He wished he had on something more easily cleaned than the two-thousand-dollar suit he'd worn to intimidate Ms. Walker. Especially since that hadn't worked very well.

He glanced to where Rosalie was still talking on the cell, her eyes fixed on the kid.

"No," he said again.

Joey lowered his arms and put one thumb in his mouth while he gave Morgan a considering look. Finally the kid pulled the thumb out far enough to say, "Goey."

Near-panic set in. Was that some kind of toilet-training talk?

When he didn't respond, the kid touched his chest, and repeated, "Goey".

"Joey?"

The kid grinned at him. Charlie's grin, but also Lillian's, when she was pleased enough with something to let her guard down.

"Morgan," he replied, pointing to himself.

"Mawg."

"Close enough for a kid who's just a few months over one."

Joey continued to beam at him. "Out."

"That would still be a no."

Again the outstretched arms. "Up?"

"Okay, we'll give that one a try."

Morgan stood and picked Joey up. He did indeed have sticky hands. Sticky hands that left shiny marks on Morgan's pristine white-silk shirt when he held the kid too close and the boy pushed away.

Sticky or not, the kid smelled sweet and milky. The urge to hold him closer again was strong, but Joey apparently wanted enough distance to be able to see this strange man's face.

The cats had appeared the minute he'd bent to pick up Joey and now sat on each side of him, outwardly unconcerned with the humans around them, but clearly on guard once again.

"Okay, you're up. Now what?" Morgan asked the mini-despot.

Joey tilted his head to one side, as if considering his options. "Tans."

Morgan made a show of scanning the toy-strewn floor of the living room. "I see lots of stuff here, but no tanning booths. And it's too cloudy outside for sun bathing. Sorry."

"Tans." Joey bounced up and down on Morgan's arm. "Sick. Tans." He reached those sticky hands up and patted Morgan's ears. "Sick. Sick."

"Music? Dance?"

"Tans!" Joey clapped his hands and bounced harder.

"Ooookay. Don't suppose you know where the remote for the sound system is."

"Sick. Tans."

"I'm working on it. Boy, this learning-to-talk thing is a bitch, isn't it?" Morgan muttered as he searched the room for some kind of remote.

"Bitch," Joey echoed perfectly.

Morgan groaned.

The remote was on the mantle over the empty fireplace, well out of reach of little hands. He shifted Joey to one hip—not as easy for him as for Rosalie—and held the remote away from the kid while he examined the controls. Finally he found what he hoped was the right button.

A wild dancing rhythm burst out of speakers on the shelves of the built-in bookcases on each side of the front window. Something familiar, yet . . .

"Tans!" Joey insisted, bouncing so much that Morgan had to set the remote back on the mantle and grab him with both arms.

Morgan took a couple of shuffling steps back and forth.

"More!"

Morgan broke into what he remembered of a waltz, although the music was much too fast and didn't have the right beat. Then he recognized it. The last movement of Brahms' double concerto. Who would have thought?

Now he knew where the music was headed, he matched his step to the rhythm, much to Joey's delight. They made two circuits of the living room before the music reached its climax.

The joy and trust on the Joey's face as they spun in one last circle stopped Morgan's heart. He'd once been that innocent, that trusting too. And so had Charlie.

In that instant he knew. He could never let Lillian, much less Charlie's father, get their hands on this kid. He had to find a way to keep Joey safe and happy.

Chapter Five

When the music stopped, Joey crowed and laughed, clapping his hands. Someone else clapped too.

Morgan cringed and looked toward the front hall. Luckily, their appreciative audience wasn't Rosalie, who had turned her back to hunch over her cell on the porch, but a skinny teenaged girl with bright-red braids

"Jill!" Joey called to her.

"Hey, Jojo, who's your hot friend?"

Morgan felt a flush creep up his face. This child thought he was hot?

He set Joey back in the playpen, grabbed the remote, and clicked off the sound system.

"You're late." He wished he'd used a softer tone when she lifted her eyebrows and stared at him.

"I just got home from soccer practice. The coach made us do extra laps 'cause some of the girls were talking instead of running the drills." The girl went over and lifted Joey out of the playpen. "Who's the hunk, kid?"

Before Morgan could explain, Rosalie came back in from the porch. Under the harried expression on her face he saw a trace of satisfaction. Her phone call must have been a success.

The red-haired girl bounced Joey and asked Rosalie, "Aren't you going to introduce me to the new boyfriend?"

"He's not . . ."

"I'm not . . ."

They'd started and stopped at the same moment.

The girl raised her eyebrows again and glanced from one of them to the other. Rosalie's face had gone pink, which for some reason made Morgan smile.

"Whatever." The girl handed the kid to Rosalie. "I don't suppose you're still going to pay me?"

Rosalie pulled a five-dollar bill out of her pocket. "You did your best. This should cover the new download you were talking about the other day."

"And then some. Thanks. I owe you. Good luck with the hottie. I think he's a keeper. He even danced with Jojo."

Rosalie gave Morgan a look that made him flush again. The girl laughed, kissed the top of Joey's head, and went out the front door.

"Obviously you need better child-care arrangements for the weekends," Morgan commented as he straightened his crumpled shirt and tightened his tie.

"Obviously you need to mind your own business. What are you doing here, anyway?"

Before he could answer, the babysitter stuck her head back in the door.

"By the way, what's that monstrosity in the SUV parked out front?"

"Monstrosity?" Rosalie asked.

The girl shrugged. "It's one of our vocab words this week. And that thing out there is ug-lee."

Rosalie couldn't tell if Morgan's face was red from anger or embarrassment.

"It's a gift for the kid from Lillian," he explained.

"Who's . . ." Jill began, but Rosalie silenced her with a glare. "Okay, I'm out of here."

The slam of the door behind her rang through the open beams of the Spanish-style living room. Rosalie took a deep breath and turned back toward her unwelcome guest.

"Why are you here?" Her heart pounded so hard she was surprised it didn't echo off the beams, too.

Joey squirmed in her arms, so she set him back in the playpen, where he plopped down and began emitting unmistakable noises from the wrong end.

Morgan gave Joey an uncomfortable look before he responded. "Perhaps if we sat down?"

She sighed, shooed the cats off the couch and sat at the end nearest Joey. Morgan took two steps toward the broken armchair, then made a mid-course correction and sat at the other end of the couch. He produced a small white plastic bag from his pocket.

"I came to get a swab from the kid so we can do a DNA test."

Rosalie frowned. "They already took one at his doctor's office and sent it to the adoption agency."

"I know. This is a private test to make sure the previous one is valid."

His pompous tone made her straighten up from the slump caused by the elderly couch.

"Valid? How could it not be valid?"

"There are ways to cheat on DNA tests."

She frowned. "How?"

"Since we don't have any DNA from the child's mother, you could have sent in any male DNA and there'd be no way for anyone to tell."

"You mean you think I'd cheat on something like that? What kind of world do you live in, Mr. Danby?"

"A world where you've already lied to me about whether Joey even existed or not. Is it that big a step to cheating in order to keep his grandmother from making a legitimate claim for him?"

67

Shame twisted through Rosalie's belly. "I see. And Joey's grand-mother sent you all the way from Boston on the off-chance I'd figured out how to beat the system on this?"

"I'm in town on business."

His words reminded her of the night of her mother's opening and the magic that had blossomed between them. She stifled a sigh.

"You seem to be here a lot."

"Danby Holding Company is in the process of acquiring an L.A. start-up."

Now he sounded like a business news soundbite.

"How nice for you. How many millions do you intend to cheat the current owners out of? Or is it billions these days?"

"I'm not here to discuss the integrity of my company's busi-ness practices."

"Oh, that's right. You're here to question my integrity."

For a minute Morgan's cool look was replaced with the heat of genuine anger, but before Rosalie could react, the mask of polite indifference was firmly back in place.

"If we could get on with this, Ms. Walker." He opened the sealed plastic bag and took out two swabs.

"Not one of those immediate-results things, is it?"

"No. It's the same lab test your doctor used. Less room for error. I'll probably need your help opening the boy's mouth."

"Good guess. He bit the nurse who did it the last time. Twice." She allowed herself a grin at the strained expression on Morgan's face. "Wouldn't you like me to change him first?"

Morgan had clearly forgotten the earlier telltale noises. "That might be a good idea."

"Would you like to do it? More uncle practice."

"Er, no."

She grinned again and picked up Joey, who had been watching them solemnly and sucking on his hand.

"We'll be a few minutes. Make yourself at home." The words

were more a reflex than an invitation, but she enjoyed the look of discomfort they brought to Morgan's face.

Such a handsome face. She sighed as she carried her precious and smelly burden out of the room.

As soon as Morgan was alone again, the cats reappeared. The one he thought was Sylvester sniffed the toes of his shoes, then lay down across his feet. The spotted one, Smudge, leapt up beside him, climbed up again to touch the black spot on his nose to Morgan's cheek, then spread himself across Morgan's lap.

Morgan started to shoo it away, but a few more white cat hairs on his black suit wouldn't make it all that much worse. Besides, the gentle rumble of the cat's purr was strangely calming.

Which reminded him of how strangely calming it had been to hold Joey, and how the kid's face had glowed with joy as they'd danced around the room.

Maybe Lillian had a point when she'd suggested he should be the one to have custody of Joey. He couldn't marry Felicity, but his stepmother wouldn't be aware of how much easier it was now for single people, even single men, to adopt a child.

Of course, he'd need to get a good nanny. One he could trust to put Joey's well-being above everything else. He wouldn't be able to travel as much on business. And it would put a severe crimp in his social life.

He was still mentally listing pros and cons when Rosalie and Joey reappeared. Red corduroy had replaced the kid's jeans and Rosalie's hair had come partway out of whatever she'd used to pull it back from her face. He stifled a sigh. Such a pretty face.

Rosalie's breath caught at the sight of Morgan on her couch, her cats spread across his feet and lap, a relaxed look on his face that didn't quite fit with his uptight businessman suit. A suit that would now be covered with white fur for the rest of the day.

The smile he gave Joey, however, set off alarm bells in her head. This man was the enemy.

"Sorry about the cats," she said. "Off the sofa, guys."

When the cats left, Smudge in the lead, she sat on the couch, a wriggling Joey in her lap.

"Okay, kid." Morgan's gentle tone tugged at Rosalie's heart a moment before it sent another cascade of alarm through her.

"Goey," Joey repeated with a wary look at the stranger.

"Yeah, Joey. Open wide."

Rosalie had to suppress a giggle when Joey clamped his mouth shut.

Morgan reached out and tickled under the boy's chin.

"You can do better than that for me, can't you, buddy?" When Joey only responded with a glare, Morgan turned to Rosalie. "A little help here?"

His air of command made her want to refuse, but what would be the point?

"Hey, big boy, how about you let your step-uncle here put two nasty swabs in your mouth and make it feel yucky?"

Morgan quirked an eyebrow at her choice of words. Luckily Joey responded to her tone of voice and smiled, but kept his mouth closed tight.

"Can you show your step-uncle how many teeth you have?"

The smile faded and Joey shook his head.

Morgan had moved closer. The heat of his body was so close to her bare arm that the musky scent of his undoubtedly expensive soap tickled her nose. Her heart beat faster. A half-forgotten warmth spread through her system. The magic of the moment when they had almost kissed reverberated through her.

Morgan's voice broke through the momentary sensual haze. "Yeah, kid, show me your chompers. Betcha only have one tooth. Is that all the teeth you have?"

Leave it to a couple of males to make this a competition. But the little mouth stayed shut.

"If you open up for your step-uncle, I'll take you to the park," Rosalie tried.

Joey shot her an indignant look, as if to ask whose side she was on, and shook his head.

Morgan stretched out one long finger and tickled Joey's tummy. The boy laughed, then gave his step-uncle a wide grin. Okay, so the man had a few good instincts with kids. Damn him.

"Okay, let's count teeth," Morgan said. "Open wider so I can get them all."

Joey opened his mouth and let Morgan take two quick swabs inside his cheek under the pretense of slowly counting his teeth.

"Wow, that's a lot of teeth for a kid your age, I bet."

Morgan's fake enthusiasm brought out all Rosalie's maternal instincts. She had to protect Joey from Morgan's, and his family's, attempts to manipulate him.

But Joey saw right through the man. "No."

Morgan frowned at the rebuke, then turned away to put the swabs back in the plastic bag.

To Rosalie's shame, the loss of his heat near her body made her shiver. She pulled Joey a little closer while their guest took a pen from the breast pocket of his suit jacket, and filled in the information on the bag.

"When will you have the results?" she asked, for lack of any other way to fill the awkward silence.

"About the same time as the other test."

All the warmth was gone from his voice. The all-business, arrogant jerk who'd walked into her office that first day was back. She could feel her hackles rise in response.

Joey whimpered at the sudden edge of ice in the air. Morgan's face softened for a moment when he looked down at the child, then the aristocratic mask was back.

71

"Once Joey's paternity is verified, you'll hear from his grandmother's lawyer."

Rosalie's heart was in her throat. "Asking for visitation rights?"

"For custody. As a blood relative, she believes her claim is stronger than yours, despite Ms. Mendelev's will."

"And you?"

"I have no interest in raising a child as a single parent."

Her heart stopped. Never in her life had she heard the words "no interest" say so clearly that the man was very interested, indeed. Why else would he think that was the question she meant to ask him? She took a deep breath and her heart chugged back to life.

"Well, I do," she told him. "I love Joey and he loves me. I'll fight Charlie's mother every step of the way on this."

"That's understood."

She rolled her eyes at the cold formality of his tone. And she'd nearly let this high-class, heartless robot kiss her!

She stood, a now-drowsy Joey on one hip. "If that's everything, Mr. Danby, it's Joey's naptime."

"Nep," Joey echoed.

Morgan stood too, his face slightly red again. "What about the gift Lillian sent?"

"The monstrosity?" Rosalie had forgotten. "Why did you leave it in the SUV?"

"I didn't want the child over-excited before I was able to get the DNA sample."

"Well, by all means, let's get him over-excited now, right before his nap."

Morgan straightened. "How was I supposed to know his schedule?"

At least he sounded like a human being now, even if a stuffy and slightly angry one.

"Why don't you bring it in?"

Whatever she might have expected Morgan to bring in from

the SUV a few minutes later, it wasn't a four-foot-high purple stuffed elephant with a raised, two-foot-long trunk and huge protruding eyes. Joey took one look at the purple giant Morgan set by his playpen, screamed with fright, and burst into tears.

The glare Rosalie gave Morgan over the ugly stuffed animal's back said more than any words could have about Lillian's common sense as a grandparent, much less a parent.

Not that he didn't agree.

He made no protest as Rosalie hustled Joey out of the room. The closing of a door cut off the last of Joey's sobs, then music drifted down the hall. Mozart.

Morgan stood and wandered around the room. The cats were back. They sat side by side, watching him from the entry with wide yellow eyes.

He paused by the bookcases on each side of the front window. They held novels popular twenty years ago and stacks of art books, all of which obviously had belonged to Rosalie's mother.

The whole house still belonged to Rosalie's mother. He could see that now. She'd been the one to decorate it with floral patterns, and no doubt planted the array of flowers outside. Rosalie had left it untouched so that nothing in this room, this house told him anything about Rosalie herself. Perhaps her bedroom . . .

He refused to let his mind wander there. What more did he need to know about the woman, anyway? She and Lillian would be at legal loggerheads for months, maybe years. The more he stayed out of it, the better it would be for his mental health—and the bottom line of Danby Holding Company.

Unless he decided to join in the legal free-for-all and try to get custody of Joey himself.

He stopped pacing and sat on the couch to mentally count the pros and cons again. He was about to reach for his cell to text himself a list when Rosalie reappeared.

"You still here?" She stood in the entry, hands on hips. "I'd

73

think you'd be half-way back to wherever you usually lurk after you released that purple nightmare on an unsuspecting world."

He shrugged. "Lillian . . ."

"Is more an idiot than an evil stepmother. I get it now. The question is, why are you on her side?"

Before he could think better of it, he told her the truth. "I'm all she has. My father died within weeks of Charlie's arrest. So she's all the family I have too, I guess."

Besides, someone needed to protect Joey from Charlie's father, but raising that specter would only complicate the conversation.

"I will not feel sorry for the woman. Nice try."

He threw back his head in exasperation and stood up to leave.

"Please take the psychedelic pachyderm with you when you go," she told him. "I don't have any place to store it until Joey is old enough not to be afraid of it."

"What the hell am I supposed to do with the damn thing?"

"Maybe you can donate it to some organization that serves older kids who might actually like it. You could throw in an extra million or two to ease the pain."

His anger faded as quickly as it had come. "What do you have against rich people?"

She sank into the armchair, her body shifted to one side to avoid the broken spring.

"Nothing. I know a lot of them, from my work and from college. Of course, I appreciated the free ride I got for the whole seven years through law school, but maybe being a charity case got to me after a while. Or . . ."

She raised laser-green eyes to his. He braced himself against the attack he saw coming.

"Or maybe I just don't like rich people who appear out of nowhere to rearrange the lives of lesser mortals who were perfectly happy with the way things were." Her eyes narrowed. "Or maybe I just don't like you."

He shook his head. That last part was a lie. He'd been there the night at the gallery and, more importantly, later at the deli. The woman found him as much a temptation as he found her, which made the charge of desire she sent buzzing along his nerves that much worse.

If she could lie, so could he. "The feeling is mutual, I assure you."

He walked toward the door, but she reached up her hand to catch his sleeve as he passed. "Don't forget your elephant."

"It was a gift for Joey. From his grandmother."

"You saw how much he loved it. Get it out of here."

She was right. He could donate it to some charity. Maybe children a bit older than Joey would enjoy it, although Morgan doubted it. He'd chip in a few thousand to ease the pain, as she'd suggested, and consider himself lucky.

When he picked up the elephant, she went to open the door.

"Goodbye, Mr. Danby."

"Goodbye, Ms. Walker."

She didn't quite slam the door behind him.

He could have sworn he saw her watching him from behind the curtains as he wrestled the elephant back into the SUV. Maybe it was wishful thinking on his part. Or maybe she just wanted to be sure both he and the damned purple elephant were good and gone.

After Morgan drove away, Rosalie half sat, half collapsed on the sofa. She had housework to do and Joey would only sleep so long, but she needed to catch her breath.

She made slow circles with her head, then rubbed her temples. Morgan Danby made her head ache. Rather, her schizophrenic reaction to the man made her head ache. One moment she was drooling over him like some lust-struck adolescent. The next moment he was an enemy sent to destroy everything she held dear. She needed to get a clearer view of who, and what, he was.

He'd said his stepmother was all the family he had. How would she feel about someone who stepped in and filled the hole being parentless had left in her life? Even if she couldn't let herself feel sorry for Charlie's mother, she could see why Morgan might.

Maybe he wasn't the enemy. Maybe he was only doing a favor for his stepmother she could have, and probably would have, hired someone else to do if he'd refused. Still, Morgan had to see that his stepmother was not the one who should raise Joey.

Then there was the way Morgan had looked at Joey this afternoon, the way he'd danced with him.

She rubbed her temples again. That hadn't been about the stepmother. That had been about him bonding with his stepbrother's child, which made him the enemy after all.

And made him all the more attractive to her. Given the way her hormones hit full force any time she was within ten feet of the man, it was no wonder he gave her a headache. He represented everything she wanted in her life—and everything she feared.

Of course, she might never see Morgan Danby again. Which would be for the best.

Still . . . she sighed as she pulled herself to her feet, and the California sun shone less brightly.

Rosalie saved the brief she was writing and glanced at the corner of her computer screen. An hour until lunch. It was Friday. Maybe she'd eat with Joey at his day-care center.

She smiled. A month since Morgan Danby's last visit, three weeks since the results of the DNA test came back and still no sign of any attempt by Charlie's mother to sue for custody.

Maybe Morgan had talked her out of it. Or maybe the woman had an attack of sanity. Whatever the reasons, each day seemed sunnier.

Rosalie tried to refocus on work, but the low rumble of male voices from the reception area was getting louder and more strident. The male receptionist and a man whose voice she didn't recognize.

She tensed. Angry ex-husbands were as much a part of any family-law practice as crying wives, but she hated the nasty confrontations ten times more.

Her office door banged open.

The older man who strode into her office was a total stranger, but there was something familiar about the football-player physique clad in an obviously hand-tailored suit and the fringe of silver-red hair that remained around his mostly bald head.

Fear propelled her to her feet and robbed her of both voice and breath before she could formulate a name.

The receptionist appeared behind the newcomer. "I'm sorry. I tried to explain you were busy, but . . ."

She swallowed and found her voice. "That's okay."

The receptionist mimed that he'd be nearby, then left and closed the door.

Her visitor took another step into the room and smiled an oily smile. "Ms. Walker?"

She nodded.

He held out a large, fleshy hand. "I'm Paul Thompson. I'm here about my grandson."

She could not make herself touch the man's hand any more than she could have made herself touch the tentacles of a jellyfish.

"I'm not sure I have anything to say to you, Mr. Thompson."

His smile widened a bit, but his eyes remained chips of pale-blue ice. Charlie's eyes. She suppressed a shudder.

Mr. Thompson pulled out the chair on the other side of the desk and sat, leaning forward into her personal space. She stepped back and fell as much as sat in her chair.

"You don't have much choice about speaking to me, Ms. Walker. Or rather, you have two choices. Tell me about my grandson now, or talk to my lawyer under oath in a deposition."

"What would you like to know?"

He leaned back to pull a smartphone out of his pocket. "Just give me his name, date of birth, place of birth, names of parents on the birth certificate, current residence, legal guardian."

"I'm touched by the personal nature of your concerns."

"He's my grandson. Isn't that personal enough for you?"

She bit her tongue against a rash of unprofessional responses and rattled off the answers to his questions while he noted them down on his phone.

He grunted when she was done. "I understand you've filed for adoption."

"Yes."

"Why? A nice-looking woman like you shouldn't be tied down with a kid without a husband to, you know, take care of you."

She couldn't tell if that was a threat or a wildly inappropriate reference to her sex life. Not that it mattered. Her whole body was already rock hard with tension.

"I love him. And it's what his mother wanted."

"What about what his father wants? Don't his wishes count for anything?"

"I'd say that killing Joey's mother, not to mention a thirty-year sentence, pretty much makes his wishes about the boy's future irrelevant."

Red crept up Mr. Thompson's face. He leaned in closer. "So Charlie overreacted when his woman walked out on him. It happens. That doesn't mean he doesn't care about his son."

Rosalie swallowed against the bile rising in her throat. "When your son was contacted about child support, he claimed Joey wasn't his."

"Maybe he wasn't sure. But the DNA test . . ."

"How do you know about that? Did Charlie's mother tell you?" *Did Morgan?*

"That bitch wouldn't give me the time of day. But I, er, have an arrangement with one of her maids." He rubbed the fingers of one hand together.

Rosalie was strangely relieved to learn only bribery was involved. She had no doubt this man was capable of much worse.

Mr. Thompson gave a low cackle. "The old broad never did have the sense to keep her mouth shut in front of the servants."

Even as Rosalie winced at the man's language, she made a mental note to let Morgan know about the leak in Lillian's household.

Except, of course, she'd probably never see or talk to Morgan again. She refocused on the problem in front of her.

"The point is that your son has not been exactly a loving parent."

"The point is that he is the child's father and his wishes should take precedence over something some dead woman wrote in a will."

Rosalie absorbed the moral body blow with a silent gasp. Luckily her mother's sickness had given her lots of practice in surviving emotional ambushes that once might have leveled her. Still, she needed to be on guard. This man was a minefield of psychological assaults.

"It's for the court to decide what's in Joey's best interest."

"And you think it's in his best interest to be raised by a single woman with a demanding job and no other financial resources? I don't want my grandson raised with that kind of unstable home life."

Anger thundered through her, but she squared her shoulders and merely said, "Again, that's for the court to decide."

"Or maybe that's it. Maybe you think you've hit some kind of mother lode with the kid. Well, let me make it perfectly clear. You adopt the kid and you'll never see a red cent of my money. Lillian's either. All of hers goes to Charlie, and I'll make sure he understands that if he gives his kid one penny, he gets nothing from me. Charlie's a smart man. He knows which side his bread is buttered on."

Yet he's not smart enough to know better than to kill people. Rosalie bit her tongue so hard she tasted blood.

Something dark and no doubt evil crossed Mr. Thompson's face.

"On the other hand, I could make it very much worth your while to drop the adoption proceedings . . ."

She shot to her feet. "No! This is not about money, as hard as it may be for you to imagine that."

He stood more slowly. "I'm not sure I like your attitude."

Fear crowded the anger out of her mind. She'd seen what Charlie did to Márya.

Mr. Thompson leaned in, hands on her desk. "You don't want to make me angry with you, Ms. Walker."

Chapter Six

Rosalie dug down deep for the courage to say, "You don't want to give a judge more reason to decide you shouldn't have custody of Joey, Mr. Thompson."

"I never laid a violent hand on my son."

"Maybe not, but you taught him it was okay to lay violent hands on women. A judge might not consider that the kind of lesson a boy should learn."

Mr. Thompson fisted his hands on the desk and bent his elbows so he was eye to eye with her. "There's nothing wrong with teaching a boy how to handle women."

"Which is why your son is doing thirty years in San Quentin."

"Damned Charlie never did have any control over his temper. I should never have let Lillian have custody of him. By the time I got him back, he was too old to learn better."

Rosalie made the mistake of letting herself relax. As soon as she loosened her shoulders, Mr. Thompson's gaze shot back to her face.

"You will let me have my grandson, Ms. Walker. One way or another."

"No, I won't." She slid her hand over and punched a button on the phone.

Thompson was too focused on intimidating her to notice. When she glared back, his face went red and he slowly lifted his hand.

Rosalie managed not to cringe, but straightened away from him.

The moment froze, suspended in time. Her heart pounded as she stared him down. Was the man smarter than his son?

Apparently he was.

"You're not worth the trouble," he muttered and lowered his hand. "I have other ways to get my grandson."

The door to her office banged open. She looked past Mr. Thompson, expecting the receptionist. Morgan Danby stood there instead, his face twisted with hatred.

Damn. Thompson had beaten him here.

Even flying in on Danby Holdings' private jet hadn't made up for the time lost before Thompson's sister could reach Lillian and warn her Thompson was on his way to L.A. to claim Joey. For the sister's sake, Morgan hoped the man never learned who'd tipped them off.

Thompson turned to face him. "You?"

Morgan pulled his eyes away from the mixture of relief and confusion on Rosalie's face to glare at the older man before he loosened the fists clenched at his side. As good as a solid right to Thompson's face might feel right now, it wouldn't to help matters.

He ignored the other man to ask Rosalie, "You okay?"

She nodded, face pale. He watched her square her shoulders with new respect.

"I think our conversation is at an end, Mr. Thompson," she said. "Please leave now."

Charlie's father glanced from one of them to the other.

"Don't think this over." He jabbed a finger in Morgan's direction. "And don't think Danby will save your bacon. All he cares about is money. Just like his old man."

Thompson strode out of the room. Rosalie skirted both her desk and Morgan to follow the older man into the reception area.

"That is Paul Thompson," she told the receptionist. "If he ever comes back, call the police."

Morgan couldn't see the receptionist's face, but he heard the anger in his tone, "Gladly."

Rosalie walked stiff-backed into the office and closed the door. Now what? Morgan wondered.

The crisis dealt with, reaction set in. Rosalie swallowed the tears of anger and fear that threatened to blind her, then turned to face Morgan, who stood frowning at her from one side of the room.

"Are you okay?" he asked again.

The compassion in his voice was too much. She took a step toward him at the same moment he moved toward her, his arm raised in silent invitation. She crossed the space between them and collapsed against the solid strength of his chest, her body shaking, her breath ragged.

He held her gingerly at first, but when she sniffed instead of bursting into tears, his arms softened around her into a gentle hug. She let her arms slide around his waist, her face relaxed against the softness of his silk shirt.

"He can't take Joey away from you," Morgan said gently. "He couldn't even get custody of Charlie back when courts were much less savvy than they are now about domestic violence. Lillian still has a protection order against him, and so does his second wife. The only reason he's never been arrested is his family's money and political pull. No judge in his right mind would hand the kid over to him. Ever."

She pushed herself away to look up at him. "He told me he got custody of Charlie back."

Morgan's face twisted back into a mask of anger again for a moment before he hid it behind the usual bland mask.

83

"Lillian voluntarily surrendered custody."

"Why did she do that?"

He took a moment to answer. "My father didn't want him in the house anymore."

"Why?" she asked again, but Morgan shook the question away. "It doesn't matter."

She suspected it mattered very much, but was weak enough to let it go for now and sink back against Morgan's chest. The warmth she felt through his suit jacket and silk shirt, the regular beat of his heart while hers still raced, the steady rise and fall of his breathing calmed her until her own body relaxed, her mind cleared.

Morgan felt Rosalie melt against him. The effort not to respond physically to the softness of her body made his jaw clench, but he needed the few minutes of calm and silence as much as she did to block out the memories that roiled through his gut.

If he closed his eyes, he could see the smirk on Charlie's face. "Sure, you big baby, you tell Lillian. She's *my* mother. She'll believe me, not you." The same smirk he'd seen on Paul Thompson's face today.

After a few minutes Rosalie straightened away from his chest, gave a last dainty sniff, and lifted her head. Without meaning to, he smiled at her.

She opened her mouth to say something, but the same lightning bolt that made him smile the moment their eyes met must have hit her too, because she snapped her mouth shut and stared at him, eyes soft with unspoken want. Not a good idea.

He forced himself to release her, carefully, so she didn't think he was rejecting the offer she probably didn't know she'd made. But the one-two punch of anger and desire had done its work. The vague plan he'd come up with on the flight to L.A. hardened into a strategy he hoped would be the best solution for all of them.

Despite what he'd told Rosalie, Paul Thompson's name and wealth carried too much weight in Boston for Morgan to be absolutely sure the man and his young third wife had zero chance of getting custody of Joey—unless a more suitable couple wanted him. He'd have to fill in the details later, but he'd find a way to make the plan work. For Joey's sake.

Rosalie stepped away and cleared her throat. Time to begin phase one of the plan.

He took a mock-casual glance at his watch.

"Can I buy you lunch?"

She frowned. "I planned to have lunch with Joey at his child care. They encourage parents to visit during the day when they can."

"You look like you need a drink more than you need to spend an hour in a room full of hungry toddlers."

"You'd be surprised," Rosalie replied, not entirely honestly. She might need a drink, but she definitely did not need to spend any more time with Morgan Danby.

Luckily he'd been too absorbed in his own thoughts while he'd held her to notice that whatever opinion her mind might have, her body wanted to do a lot more than have lunch with him. Her nipples stood at full alert behind the handy armor of her jacket, and her head still spun from the rush of blood to other, more vulnerable, parts of her body.

The man might as well wear a flashing red light on his head— he was danger in a hand-tailored suit. Especially this gallant, kind, and generally swoonworthy version of him.

"You look pretty shaken." His rich baritone made her toes want to curl. "You might want to wait until you've calmed down before you see the kid again. No reason to upset him."

She hadn't thought of that, but saw no reason to admit it to him.

"I practice family law. I've been threatened before." Although never by someone with a history like Paul Thompson's. "And I

85

probably will be again. We have an office protocol for when it happens."

"You sure do. I practically had to fight my way past your receptionist to get in here."

"Nice to know the system works."

Morgan gave a rueful grin, then cocked his head to one side.

"Okay, don't have lunch with me because you need to. Have lunch with me because you want to."

"I don't want to," she lied.

Morgan took a deep breath. Her nerves tingled, but not in a good way. She wasn't going to like what he said next.

"We need to talk. I hoped lunch would make it easier."

"Make what easier?"

But she already knew.

"Telling you that Lillian's about to file for custody of Joey."

Rosalie went very still. Morgan wished he'd found a gentler way to get her to have lunch with him, but she was far too wary of him. Maybe with good reason.

When she didn't say anything, he added, "I saw a Italian place down the street."

She gave herself a little shake. "Carmelo's." Her voice had the hollow ring of resignation. "They have great food. Not fancy, but . . ."

"Not fancy is fine. Let's go. Maybe we can beat the lunch-hour rush."

Carmelo's homey atmosphere was exactly what Morgan needed. Nothing here to raise the barriers Rosalie usually kept between them. Just good, homemade pasta and a mellow glass of drinkable red wine.

He made polite chitchat through the antipasto and offered a second glass of wine, which Rosalie predictably refused. While they waited for their pasta, he could see the wheels in her mind turning. He hoped her train of thought didn't veer too far from where he wanted it to go.

"I can understand now why helping your stepmother get custody of Joey might have seemed like a good idea, if Paul Thompson was the alternative." She shuddered and took another sip of her wine. "Is that why she wants him?"

"In part, but at base her reasons are much more selfish."

He felt the first line of the barriers between them lock back into place.

"Since I never heard from her lawyer," Rosalie said, "I thought maybe she'd given up. Unless the laws are different in Massachusetts than they are in California, she can't have much chance of winning."

"That's what her regular attorney told her, but she hired a friend's nephew, fresh out of law school, who squeaked past the bar exam and agreed to take the custody case."

Rosalie looked away. He heard the clunk as the second line of barriers closed.

"I wish I could say you don't have to worry about Lillian," he said, "but I can't. She's decided I'm on your side now, and won't discuss it with me."

Rosalie's gaze zeroed back in on his face. "Are you on my side?"

Unwilling to tip his hand, he shook his head. "Consider me a friendly neutral."

"So why are you here?" She stopped and held up one hand. "Never mind. I can guess. You're in town on business."

At least her attitude was back. He'd decided he liked curvy women with attitude.

He leaned in a little closer, pleased she didn't move away. She smelled of wine and hot peppers and some flowery perfume. He might never have smelled anything sexier.

"Actually, no. I wanted to stop Thompson before he got here. My timing was a bit off."

"How did you know he was here?"

"Not everyone he trusts is blind or stupid enough to trust him."

She nodded. "Unfortunately, your stepmother has a similar problem."

When he frowned, she explained what Thompson had said about Lillian's soon-to-be-unemployed maid. By the time she finished, the server had appeared with their food.

"Have you decided on a college yet?" Rosalie asked the young woman.

The server grinned. "Got a scholarship to the University of Southern California, like you."

"Congratulations. You'll be a lawyer in no time."

The exchange lightened Rosalie's mood enough for her make a little "um" sound after she tasted her spaghetti with roasted tomatoes and garlic. Time to pick up where he'd left off.

"Stopping Thompson and telling you what Lillian is up to weren't the only reasons I'm here."

"Oh?"

"No." Morgan paused for added effect. "I'm also here to ask you out."

She froze. Had he blown it?

He held his breath until she stabbed at her spaghetti with her fork. "Very funny."

"I'm serious."

She set the fork down and sighed.

"Do I need to list the reasons why (a) you can't want to ask me out, (b) I can't want to go out with you, and (c) it's a crazy idea in and of itself, no matter what either of us wants?"

He pulled back. "This isn't a courtroom. I don't need you to write me a legal brief with bullet points."

"Call it a reality check, then. And it isn't so different from a courtroom. You are trying to make a case."

"There is no try. I *am* making a case. I want to get to know

88

you." He ticked each point off on his fingers. "You're attracted to me."

He paused, but she looked away rather than deny it. A good sign.

"And I already told you I'm a neutral party in your conflict with Lillian."

The shuttered expression on her face told him it was time to bring out the big guns and let her see one of the real reasons behind his invitation.

"No, not neutral," he corrected. "Not really, I'm on Joey's side. Go out with me and prove that puts me on your side, too."

Normally, he avoided emotional blackmail at all costs. He'd grown up in a hotbed of it. But nothing was normal about this situation. He needed to break through those barriers and Lillian hadn't given him much time to do it.

Besides, it'd worked. He had Rosalie taking the idea seriously.

Before she could come up with more excuses not to take him up on his offer, he lifted his hand to tuck one finger under her chin and tilt her face up until their eyes met.

"Will you go out on a date with me?"

She gazed at him for a moment before she pulled away. "Who'll take care of Joey?"

"Who usually watches him when you go out on a date?"

"I don't date. I've never dated much."

The wistful tone in her voice made him want to comfort her again. The impulse should have scared him silly, but he didn't have time to think about it. He needed to get the conversation back on track to the next stage of his plan. Still, her reaction gave him a clue on where to start.

"It must have been hard to have so much responsibility all those years."

The pang of sympathy behind his words was more real than he'd expected.

"My mother was pretty independent, until near the end."

"You've spent so much of your life taking care of people," he said with genuine admiration. "Your mother, now Joey. A lot of women would resent the kind of sacrifices you've made."

She shook her head. "It's not a sacrifice if you love someone."

Not something he'd had the chance to learn one way or the other. "But you didn't even have time to date."

"It never seemed important to me."

"It can't be that you don't like men."

She lifted an eyebrow. "Can't it?"

"No. We have too much sexual chemistry between us."

She started to interrupt, but he didn't give her the chance.

"Don't try to deny it. Why else would I fly over two thousand miles to ask you out?"

Their eyes met, heating the air between them again to confirm his words.

"Because you have a backhanded plan to take Joey away from me?"

Her distrust stung, the more so because of how close it came to the truth.

"No—a backhanded plan to get to know you better."

"I told you, I don't date."

The words came out harsher, colder than Rosalie intended. Even the word "date" set her nerves on edge. She'd dated enough to learn there wasn't much point to it. After all, the purpose of dating was to fall in love, and love meant trusting a man. But men always walked, the way her father had. The way her one serious boyfriend in college had once he figured out her mother was more important to Rosalie than fraternity parties or ski weekends.

"If you don't date, how do you begin a relationship?"

"I don't want a relationship. I'm happy with my life the way it is."

Brave words, but his knowing smile reminded her of how good it felt to be in his arms.

She was far too vulnerable to this man. She needed to get him out of her life before she did something stupid, like care about him. Or trust him.

She gave him a long, cool look. "And if I did want a relationship, you'd be the last man on my list."

Which was true. The attraction she felt for him, the deeper feelings he'd begun to arouse in her were far too dangerous. But he did as she'd hoped and took her words with a very different meaning. A sharp light sparked in his eyes.

"Given your attitude, I have to wonder whether, if Lillian wants Joey for a motherhood do-over, you want him because otherwise you'll never be able to have a child."

His angry blast hit too close to home. She shot to her feet.

"So this was all about Joey after all! Well, you can go to hell, Morgan Danby."

Morgan absorbed Rosalie's attack. He deserved it. But he couldn't let her leave now. He reached out and caught her hand to stop her.

A jolt of white-hot need arced through him at the contact. Her eyes went wide with surprise, as if it burned her too. She didn't pull away, but stared down at him, tiny quivers in her fingers the sole clue to how torn she was.

He released her hand. "I'm sorry. That was unforgivable, but please forgive me and stay."

She hesitated for a moment before she sat again, the familiar wariness back on her face.

He reached for her hand, but she jerked it away and put it under the table.

"I did come here to ask you out on a date," he began. "I can't believe you'd say no just because you've dated some jerks in the past."

She paled, opened her mouth, then closed it.

Oh, yes. The problem wasn't the jerks she'd dated, but the mega-jerk who'd walked out on her and her sick mother.

"We don't have to call it a date," he hurried on to fill in the awkward moment. "Call it two people who enjoy each other's company spending time together. What do you say?"

Rosalie fought to hold herself together. Literally. She felt split in two by her simmering anger and wariness of Morgan on one side, and the way her body still chimed from his touch, the undeniable chemistry, as he'd put it, between them. To go out with him would be to submit herself to an evening of emotional ping pong.

"No," she repeated, more to herself than to him. "I can't."

"What if we made it a three-way date?"

How many glasses of wine did he drink?

"What?"

He laughed. "I mean you, me, and Joey. If we take him to the zoo, say, I'd have chance to get to know him, and you'd have a chance to learn for yourself what a great guy I am."

"I don't think . . ."

"The problem is, you think too much." The almost-fond look on his face took the sting out of his words. "You need to relax and let go a little now and then. Go to the zoo with me and Joey tomorrow. It'll do you good. You might even enjoy it."

How could she enjoy anything with Morgan around? He stirred desires she'd forgotten she had, raised hopes and fears she'd thought she'd long since gotten past.

She started to shake her head, then remembered how he'd lured her to lunch. Lillian had decided to file for custody of Joey. Much more was at stake than Rosalie's battered heart.

She took another bite of her pasta to buy time.

Nothing sexual was about to happen between them with Joey in tow. While Morgan tried, for some inexplicable reason, to charm her into a real date, she'd be able to use the time to do what he'd suggested she do, win him over to her side, get him to talk his stepmother into dropping the custody suit.

She drained the last of her wine. "The zoo might work. We haven't been there recently."

"Should I pick you up?"

"No." She'd need a way to escape if he stepped the least little bit over the line. "We'll meet you there. What time?"

"Eleven?"

"Ten would give us more time before lunch and nap."

"Sure."

"I'll see you then." She pushed her chair back and reached for her purse.

He stood when she did. For a moment she was afraid he might touch her or volunteer to walk her back to her office. She needed to get away from him and regroup. She needed to get away from him, period.

Maybe he could read the urge to flee on her face, because he took a step back and gave a casual wave. "Bye."

Joey was not in a good mood the next morning. Only the promise of a car ride prevented a full-scale tantrum while Rosalie tried to get him dressed. She didn't tell him about the zoo until he got fussy after the drive there stretched out beyond his willingness to sit in his car seat.

"Nals!" he burbled. "Now!"

She turned off the freeway, well aware of the traffic around Griffith Park on a Saturday and how long it might be before they actually saw any "nals."

A cloudy sky had kept enough people away that the parking lot wasn't full. She pulled into a space near the entrance and began the laborious process of unloading Joey's gear, keeping up a one-sided conversation with him through the open car window so he didn't fuss.

"Giraffes and hippos and elephants and . . ." she recited as she wrestled with the stroller.

Strong hands took the unwieldy mass of metal and plastic from her and effortlessly flipped it open.

"And monkeys," Morgan picked up her litany, "and tigers."

Rosalie gasped and put one hand to her chest, where her heart beat wildly, then realized she must look like an old-fashioned heroine with the vapors.

"You startled me." She reached into the trunk for the diaper bag.

Morgan reached for the cooler at the same moment. Their shoulders bumped. Her heart beat went from wild to frenzied, but she managed to pull away without letting on how much his presence affected her.

"How did you spot us?" she asked as they stowed the various bags and bundles in the stroller's compartments.

"This old Saab is like a billboard that flashes 'frugal parent of a small child' in neon lights. Hard to miss."

She went to get Joey out of his car seat, glad for the chance to take a few full breaths.

"You need an SUV with all this stuff," Morgan went on.

She settled Joey in the stroller and strapped him in.

"They use too much gas. Not good for the environment, or the pocket book."

"They make hybrid SUVs these days."

He took the handle of the stroller and pushed it toward the entrance to the zoo while she slammed the trunk shut.

"Not in my budget. Especially now I have a custody battle to fight."

The reminder made her hurry to follow them, uneasy with leaving Joey in his step-uncle's care even for a moment. What if he was still on his stepmother's side after all?

Morgan must have sensed her reaction, because he let go when she grabbed the stroller and gave her a wry smile that made her pulse jump back to double time.

Rosalie was dismayed to discover that, despite the partly empty parking lot, there was a substantial line to buy tickets at the zoo entrance.

Joey was in no mood to sit and wait. Once they were in a crowd, where all he could see were legs and feet, he started to fuss.

"I'll walk him around," Rosalie told Morgan, who nodded.

The plaza around the entrance was dotted with other parents pushing other fussy toddlers in strollers. Older children lingered around the souvenir and snack shops. Joey took it all in, wide-eyed but blessedly quiet.

Until he saw the balloon man.

"Me! Me!" He bounced up and down in the stroller.

"I don't think so." Rosalie swallowed a wistful sigh. She'd always loved balloons. "Balloons break and make a big noise."

"Balloons are so sad," she'd heard her mother say again and again over the years. "They waste away to ugly little lumps of rubber. Not like flowers."

Flowers are alive and die, Rosalie had always wanted to protest. She hadn't, of course, but a little part of her still wanted the balloon she never got.

"Me! Me!" Joey continued, well on the way to a tantrum.

Morgan came up with their tickets. "Me what?"

"He wants a balloon." This time she did sigh.

"What color?"

He reached for his wallet, but she stopped him.

"It'll just break."

"So what? He'll enjoy it while he has it, and if it breaks, he'll learn something about brightly colored objects."

The balloon man had noticed them.

"I love to see a happy family," he called with a grin. "For you, two balloons for the price of one."

Rosalie couldn't resist a smile at the thought of two balloons bouncing around her house.

Morgan must have read more into the smile than she meant him to, because he strode over to the man and handed him a bill.

"What colors?" the man asked.

Morgan looked down to where Joey watched him from the stroller, hand in his mouth.

"Blue for Joey." He turned to Rosalie. "What color do you want yours to be?"

"Mine? I don't . . ."

"You know you want one. What color?"

At the very top of the bunch of balloons sat a single golden-yellow one, the color of a summer sun. Afraid to trust her voice, she pointed at it.

The balloon man pulled out the right two strings and gave them to Morgan.

Joey chuckled and clapped his hands. Rosalie couldn't stop herself from beaming as Morgan ceremoniously handed her the string to the golden balloon.

"Give your hubby a kiss to thank him." The balloon man's grin grew wider.

Rosalie felt her face go red. "He's not my hub—husband."

"Even more reason to give him a good one, lady."

Chapter Seven

Morgan joined in the man's laughter while Rosalie pretended to be absorbed in the tricky task of tying the balloons to the stroller—Joey's to the front, where he could see it, hers to the handle.

Once that was done they joined the flow of parents and children, and an occasional young couple with stars in their eyes, through the gate to the zoo.

Joey was as entranced by the crowds of people and other toddlers in strollers as he was by the animals. Morgan used the map to guide them to the larger, easily seen, species Joey was most likely to recognize.

The crowd around the elephants proved too dense to move through, so Morgan unclicked Joey from the stroller before Rosalie realized what he was doing, and swung the child up to his shoulders. Joey giggled and bounced up and down on his perch, more thrilled to be way up high than at the sight of the huge, gray beasts.

They moved on to the lion exhibit with him still on Morgan's shoulders. Joey loved the ride, but when one of the lions gave a huge roar for the audience, he screeched and reached for Rosalie. She took the familiar weight from Morgan and swung Joey a few times side to side like a baby to calm him before she put him back in the stroller.

Morgan glanced at his watch. He had on a red designer polo shirt today with sharply creased chinos that put Rosalie's unironed black trousers and flowered blouse to shame.

"Lunchtime?" he asked her with a nod toward Joey, who looked as if he was deciding whether to fuss or not.

"Good plan."

"Shall we try the Children's Zoo after lunch?" Morgan asked while they waited in line.

Rosalie shook her head. "He'll need a nap after all the excitement."

"We'll do the Children's Zoo next time."

She started to protest that there wouldn't be a next time, but they'd reached the front of the line and Morgan had turned his attention to ordering their meal.

She told him what she wanted and guided Joey's stroller to a table near the windows.

When Morgan joined them a few minutes later, she was shocked to see what he'd bought for Joey.

"A hot dog! He might choke."

"I thought you could take it out of the bun and he'd be able to hold it and chew on it."

"They used to think it was okay, but not anymore. Bites of hot dog are just the right size to get caught in a toddler's throat. Besides they're full of fat and . . ."

"If a guy's uncle can't spoil him, who can?" Morgan gave her a heart-stopping grin.

"Step-uncle," she corrected, to deflect it.

Instead of handing her the hot dog, he unwrapped it, took the meat out of the bun, and carefully cut the sausage into small pieces with the white plastic knife that came with the food.

Once he had a few pieces cut, he set them on a napkin in front of Joey, who sniffed the unfamiliar food for a moment before he took an experimental bite. Pure pleasure lit his face as he chewed the salty, fatty meat.

"I'll never get him to eat puréed liver again."

Morgan laughed. "You owe me, kid," he told Joey, who giggled back at him.

As Morgan continued to cut up the hot dog and put the pieces on the napkin for Joey, Rosalie's breath caught at the realization that Morgan cared about her little boy.

Her heart broke into a crazy, almost painful, dance at the twin realization that she cared about Morgan, too. How could she not when he fed Joey, helped her scare off Paul Thompson, and made her laugh?

No. She didn't dare feel anything for this man. The lust he inspired in her was bad enough. She mentally added alarm bells to the red lights she tried to see every time she looked at Morgan.

In fact, it was worse if he liked Joey. If he'd hated "the kid," he wouldn't want him around in the stepmother's life.

Much too late it hit her. She'd messed up big time. Instead of winning Morgan over to her side in the custody dispute with the zoo trip, she'd pushed him in the other direction. Joey's adorableness had undermined her plan.

Morgan hid a smug smile. The plan was right on course.

Joey fell asleep as soon as Rosalie changed his diaper after lunch so they walked back to the car in silence. Once there, Morgan held the stroller steady to make it easier for her to undo the straps and lift Joey into his car seat without waking him.

Morgan collapsed the stroller while she buckled Joey in, then waited for her to unlock the trunk to stow all the paraphernalia inside.

The two balloons bobbing out of the open trunk reminded him of the expression on her face earlier. He didn't know what was behind her reluctance to let him buy her a balloon, or her delight when he did, but it reinforced his sense that staying at home to take care of her mother all those years had deprived Rosalie of more than experience with men. No matter how much her mother tried to prevent it, between her needs and the grades required to keep those scholarships, Rosalie couldn't have much time to find her own way in life.

Valuable information. Still, he had to be careful. She didn't need, and wouldn't want, him to feel sorry for her, any more than she needed, or wanted, him to lust after her, but both reactions felt more and more inevitable to him.

Even now, with her hair loose around her face and her clothes disheveled from moving Joey from stroller to car, he had to fight to keep erotic images of other reasons her hair and clothing might be in disarray out of his mind.

The slam of the car door shook him back to reality. Now for the next phase of the plan.

"Do you have to rush home?" he asked her.

She shook her head, a puzzled look on her face.

"I thought maybe we could talk."

Puzzled became suspicious. "About what?"

He leaned back against the side of the car parked next to hers and crossed his arms, unwilling to contemplate why this conversation had his gut twisted in a tight knot around the over-cooked hamburger he'd had for lunch.

"About how, now you know I'm a nice guy, we should go out on a date, the two of us."

She leaned back against her car, her arms crossed in unconscious imitation of his.

"Why should we?"

"Because it might be fun?" He let his smile fade a bit. "How often in your life have you done anything just for fun?"

"I have fun all the time." She glanced into the car at Joey, her face wistful. "Joey has brought so much joy to my life."

100

"I'm sure, but doing something simply for fun is different from when you have fun doing what you have to do anyway or doing what makes someone else happy."

"So I should have fun going out with you because it will make you happy?"

The knot in his gut tightened another notch. The woman was too damn smart. Usually he found that attractive, but right now he'd settle for a less sharp edge on her brain.

"You don't have to make me happy."

Seeing you happy would be enough.

Where the hell did that come from? He pushed the question away to focus on his main goal.

"Have dinner with me Tuesday night and . . ."

She shook her head. "I have to be in court Wednesday morning."

He hid a smile at the telltale sign she took his invitation more seriously than she let on.

"Wednesday night, then. We can celebrate your victory in court."

"Highly unlikely. My client cheated on his wife with his secretary and now wants full custody of the kids."

The word "custody" hung in the air between them.

"So why did you agree to represent him?" he asked to distract her.

"I do all the legal work for the chain of dry cleaners he owns, so I didn't feel like I could turn him down when he asked me to represent him in the divorce. I think they'll reconcile before it's over, anyway. The wife is nuts about him, and he knows he made a terrible mistake. He's broken it off with the secretary and transferred her to another location."

"What if I buy you dinner Wednesday night to console you for your loss in court?"

"You like to win, don't you?"

He raised an eyebrow. "You say that like it's a bad thing."

"Maybe not in business, but I'm not sure it bodes well for a dinner date."

"Why not give it a try and see?"

They were back in court, Rosalie realized, with Morgan making a case, or trying to. She was the one who had to decide on a verdict, but how?

An exercise from her legal writing class floated into her mind. "Visualize your argument as a flow chart," the instructor had told them. It helped her write successful briefs. Maybe it'd help her decide now.

Her goal was clear—end the custody battle. Her immediate choice was to go to dinner with Morgan or not. What she needed were the links to take her from here to there.

If she said no, and if Morgan didn't hold a grudge, things would stay more or less how they were now. He'd stay neutral, and she was on her own with the lawsuit. If he did hold a grudge, she'd be slightly worse off with regard to the legal battle, but his allegiance was worth a lot more to her than it was to his step-mother.

If she said yes, she had a chance to win big. The mistake she'd made with the zoo trip was to ignore the possibility of Morgan getting attached to Joey. But without her adorable boy around, that risk was eliminated. She'd have the perfect opportunity to win Morgan over to her side, the way she'd planned to do in the first place. Problem solved.

Except it wasn't. Life wasn't a courtroom, or a logic problem. Last time she didn't pay enough attention to Morgan's emotions. This time she needed to be careful to pay enough attention to her own.

He lounged against the car, his dark hair wind-tossed, no longer the powerful businessman who'd bought her lunch the day before, although the pure masculinity that had made her afraid he'd pound Paul Thompson to a pulp in her office still shimmered around him. How he'd acted with Joey today added allure to the complex person she'd begun to see under his win-at-all-costs façade. He'd turned out to be a good guy after all.

The alarm bells went off in her head. In this case, "good guy" was not good. She was far too attracted to him. If she ignored the attraction, however, and shifted the balance so his power worked in her favor and against his stepmother, she would be that much closer to permanent custody of Joey. And Joey was what mattered most.

She was an intelligent adult. She'd done harder things than resist Morgan Danby's undeniable sex appeal for a few hours. If her heart got a little bruised in the process, she could handle it. With a little luck, maybe she'd find a way to turn the situation into a game of wits. It might even be fun.

She looked up into his eyes and her throat went dry. Some wild spark deep inside told her it might also be the most exciting night of her life.

Morgan watched the wheels go around in Rosalie's head and hid his impatience with the woman-whisperer smile he'd perfected at an early age.

When a beep from the car he'd been leaning against signaled the approach of the people who owned it, he straightened and moved into Rosalie's personal space. Her eyes widened and her gaze dropped to her toes.

Which were painted a sexy poppy-red. Why the hell had he noticed that?

"Well?" he asked.

"Yes."

It came out more a sigh than a word, so it took a moment to register in Morgan's mind. Now he'd won, he stepped back to give her more space. "Seven o'clock, Wednesday?"

"Will you still be in town?"

"I own the company. I can be where I want to be when I want to be there, and I want to be in L.A. on Wednesday to take you to dinner."

"I can't stay out too late. Joey's an early riser."

"I'll have you home at a reasonable hour. I promise."

"Um, okay. I—I have to get going before Joey wakes up."

He stepped toward her and kissed her on the forehead.

"I'll see you Wednesday."

She looked up at him, a mixture of surprise, pleasure, and panic written on her face.

"Okay," she breathed again.

He walked away before she pulled herself together enough to change her mind.

Rosalie felt like a raw amateur who'd gone ten rounds with the heavyweight champ. She gave herself a little shake and got in the car. Luckily, Joey slept the whole way home, then played in his playpen while she did chores and tried to shut what she'd done out of her mind.

After Joey was in bed for the night, she allowed herself the luxury of calling Vanessa to tell her about the dinner with Morgan. She took a sip of mint tea and pushed the button on her cell next to Vanessa's perfect face.

"What do you plan to wear on your first date in years?" was her friend's predictable first question. "Not one of your flowery dresses, I hope."

"It's not a date! And what's wrong with flowers?"

"Haven't you figured out yet that flowers are so not you? Flowers are all 'I'm bright and pretty', and you're all 'I'm quiet and deep.' Do you have anything blue you could wear?"

"I have a pale-blue chambray sundress with the buttons up the front."

"Perfect. Men go crazy over all those little buttons."

Something hot and sweet blossomed low in Rosalie's belly.

She closed her eyes against the images that flooded her mind. "I won't let him unbutton them."

She could almost hear Vanessa roll her eyes.

"Of course not. But the possibility you might will still drive him crazy."

"How do you know?"

"Who's married to the greatest guy in the world?"

Normally Rosalie would have responded "You are" without a moment's hesitation. But although Aaron was a great guy, he wasn't as good with Joey as Morgan was. Aaron didn't understand her well enough to get under her skin, the way Morgan did. Aaron's smile didn't make her knees go weak, the way Morgan's did.

"What have I gotten myself into?" she said, more to herself than to Vanessa.

"Hey, don't overthink this. Relax and have a little fun. You deserve it."

"Do you realize how long it's been since I was on a date?"

"I thought it wasn't a date, just dinner with a friend."

"Morgan isn't my friend," Rosalie responded automatically.

"So why did you agree to go out with him?"

"I thought it'd give me a chance to get him to talk his step-mother into dropping the custody suit."

"So this is all about Joey, huh?" Vanessa's tone was skeptical. "Then why does this guy want to have dinner with you?"

As if Rosalie hadn't already asked herself that a thousand times. "I don't know."

"It couldn't be because you're an attractive, intelligent woman with a warm heart and a great sense of humor?"

"Maybe."

Vanessa gave a un-supermodel-like snort. "Dress up so you look great, but are still comfortable. Relax and try to have a good time. Don't let the man steamroller you. Do you think you can do that?"

105

"Probably."

"Only probably?"

It was an old game from their law-school days, invoked whenever one of them had a big exam or a paper due. It'd gotten them both through the bar exam and sped Vanessa through her CPA exams.

"Definitely. I can do that," Rosalie replied with a laugh.

I can do that, she repeated to herself as she ironed around the buttonholes on the blue chambray dress on Wednesday evening, but the images of Morgan undoing all those buttons to expose the sensitive flesh of her breasts teased at the edges of her mind.

She grabbed the dress and turned off the iron. When she glanced into the living room to check on Joey in his playpen, the half-deflated yellow balloon on the mantle nodded at her, a cheery reminder of Morgan's kindness, his sensitivity to what she wanted, needed . . .

Not a good thing to remember right now. She needed to stay focused on Joey and the custody battle.

But the image of Morgan's hands on her body followed her into her bedroom.

In the end, the practical white bra went back into the drawer. Instead she pulled out the pale-blue lace one she'd bought on a whim the same day she'd bought the sundress. To bolster her ego. After that it was easy to put on the matching lace panties. She added a simple white half-slip and buttoned herself into the dress. Morgan was due in less than five minutes.

Morgan arrived at Rosalie's house five minutes early. He sat in the car and wondered why until it was time to walk the flower-lined path to her door.

Through the wide windows to the dining room he saw Rosalie in the kitchen doorway talking to someone. She wasn't wearing a flowered dress this time, but a blue one that outlined the soft curves of her body.

106

A wave of primal emotion demanded he take his time with this woman, make her completely his at the slow, deliberate pace she deserved.

But Lillian had taken the time he needed away from him.

He stepped back and pressed the doorbell. Rosalie frowned as she crossed the dining room, both cats in her wake. Would she try to back out at the last minute?

Before he could come up with a Plan B if she did, she swung the door open, a bright smile on her face.

Startled, he took a moment before he grinned back at her.

"Hi." With practiced expertise she lifted one foot to block the cats.

He focused for a moment on the bare toes revealed by her sandals before he traced a leisurely visual path up her legs to the billowy skirt of her dress. His body jumped to full attention when his gaze moved higher to all the little buttons that shaped her lush breasts.

"Come on in and say hello to Joey."

The breathless, wispy quality in her voice made his heart pump. He looked into her eyes, amazed to see the same kind of heat there.

The kid. Think about the kid. The flowery scent of her perfume made it difficult, but he fixed his mind on the long-term goal and followed her through the kitchen to the breakfast room.

The small room's wide bay window opened on the backyard, where a grassy space had been cleared for a toddler play set between the driveway and another lavish garden of flowers. An evening breeze stirred the swing that hung from the branch of a large pepper tree.

The older lady from across the street sat at the round breakfast table next to the highchair. Apparently it did take a village to raise a child, at least for a single mom.

The spoon the older lady held stopped in midair at Joey's joyful cry of "Mawg!" Her bright-blue eyes peered up at Morgan through trifocal lenses, then moved to Rosalie's face. The woman gave a nod—of approval, he hoped—and stuck the spoon in Joey's open mouth.

Rosalie made the introductions. When Morgan sat on the other side of the highchair for a moment to talk to Joey, the cats took their guardian positions on each side of him.

"Hey, kid, how was your day?"

"He had a very good day," Rosalie answered. "He had fun at day care, and I got home early enough for a walk before dinner. Now he has Mrs. Peterson to spoil him."

The older woman's back straightened. "I do not spoil him."

Rosalie smiled. "No, of course not." She stepped closer, too close to Morgan to whisper loudly enough for the sitter to hear her, "She lets him watch cartoons until he falls asleep."

Mrs. Peterson reddened as she spooned what looked like stew into Joey's mouth.

Morgan worked to keep his mind on the byplay between the women despite the fact that every nerve in his body had gone on alert the moment Rosalie's breath tickled his ear.

He swallowed and stood. "I'm afraid we have to go. Our reservation's for eight."

Rosalie bent to give Joey a hug and kiss goodbye. To Morgan's surprise, she led him at a quick pace to the front door.

"The sooner we're gone, the less time Joey will have to decide to fuss," she explained in a low voice and shut the door quietly behind them.

He gave what he hoped was a knowing nod and took her arm below the light shawl she'd thrown around her shoulders. The skin-on-skin contact seared and comforted him at the same time. Which made no sense, but felt right.

So far so good. If he kept his mind on the plan . . .

It could be a long evening.

It promised to be a long evening. Morgan had on a tailored white-linen jacket with a pale-green shirt and a plain pair of black trousers. Despite her best efforts, Rosalie couldn't help but wonder how he would look shirtless, how his muscles would feel if she touched them, how his skin would feel if she kissed it. Not a good sign.

Why did Morgan Danby have to be the one man who filled her mind with images of naked bodies tangled on pristine beaches and branded her body with X-rated wants and impulses?

He clicked open the doors of the upmarket German hybrid he'd rented this time and helped her in before he went around the front to climb in beside her.

During the ride out to the beach they discussed the famous sights they passed. She was surprised by how well he knew L.A. He even seemed to share her enthusiasm for the city, despite its less-than-stellar reputation as a place to live or raise a child.

When they reached the restaurant, the gorgeous blonde at the desk inside the door told them they'd have a half-hour wait for their table, despite their reservation.

Morgan started to protest, but Rosalie saw the hottest couple in Hollywood sneak past them—dark sunglasses still in place in the dimly lit restaurant—and elbowed him into silence.

"What was that about?" he asked after they ordered drinks in the restaurant bar.

"It's Malibu. The very rich and very famous get priority over the merely very rich."

"In Boston, we have proper respect for sheer wealth."

"In Boston you don't have to live in a fish bowl like those people do."

The server brought a single-malt whiskey, neat, for Morgan, and a ruby-red Cabernet for her. She held the fruity richness of the wine on her tongue for a moment before she let it slide down her throat, lighting tiny flares of delight on the way.

Morgan took a healthy drink of his whiskey. "So, how did court go today?"

"Pretty much the way I expected."

She looked at him for signs he wasn't interested, but his eyes stayed on her face and he nodded to encourage her. So she sketched him an account of how the case had played out, then filled it in as he asked all the right questions. She stumbled over some of her words, unused to sharing the ups and downs of her day with anyone except Joey, but Morgan showed none of the signs of impatience his young nephew usually did.

Eventually they were shown to a table near the window, not far from the Hollywood couple, who talked in low tones over their food, refusing to make eye contact with anyone.

After they ordered, Rosalie asked about the L.A. start-up Morgan wanted to acquire.

"You can't really be interested in that."

"If I wasn't interested, I wouldn't have asked."

He shrugged and launched into a summary of why his company had its eye on this particular technology.

The server brought their food half-way through the story. Rosalie inhaled the sweet-tangy steam hovering over her bouillabaisse. Morgan's mixed seafood grill added an earthier undertone that reminded her how long it'd been since she'd gobbled a sandwich outside the courthouse.

They ate in companionable silence at first, but once her initial hunger eased, she asked Morgan all the questions she'd thought of while he talked about the start-up.

She'd never wanted a career in business law, but had enjoyed the mergers and acquisitions course she took. To hear how the theories she'd learned worked in practice was an eye-opener, especially given Morgan's insight and enthusiasm, and his willingness to answer her questions.

Every now and then she'd remind herself to take a bite of her meal and get distracted by the little explosions of tomato, herbs, and perfectly cooked seafood on her tongue.

Once the topic of the start-up was exhausted, they moved on to other business deals he considered key to his company's success and the other cases she was working on. The conversation had all the excitement of the best late-night sessions from law school, with the added spice of the simmering sexual attraction between them. She wasn't sure she'd ever enjoyed a conversation more.

By the time they'd finished the restaurant's signature low-fat dessert of lemon-ice sorbet and angel food cake, she looked up to discover the place was half empty.

"What time is it?" She reached into her purse for her cell. "Ten-thirty! Mrs. Peterson will think something awful has happened."

Morgan smiled. "Call her and tell her you're having a wonderful time and will be home later than you expected."

Mrs. Peterson didn't sound surprised at all when Rosalie called.

"I'll bed down on the couch if I get sleepy. Stay out all night, if you like."

Rosalie felt color creep up her cheeks. She asked how Joey was and added, "Call me if you need me," before she hung up.

Morgan shifted his gaze from the waves on the beach below them. "You are having a wonderful time, aren't you?"

"Yes. Are you terribly bored?"

Morgan couldn't have been less bored. Or more frustrated.

The frustration wasn't just sexual, although that was there in spades. Every time Rosalie took a bite of her bouillabaisse and her face went soft with sensual pleasure, his body throbbed.

At the same time, his mind rebelled against the need to rush past the unexpected delight of exploring this woman's mind. If he moved too fast with her, he'd put whatever might have naturally grown between them at risk. He hadn't accomplished what he had in life without a few major risks, but he wasn't sure this one was worth the price. Except Joey would be the big loser if Morgan didn't act fast.

"No, I'm not bored," he said. "How about a walk on the beach?"

Chapter Eight

Rosalie blinked twice and opened her mouth to say no, Morgan was sure, before she closed it with a soft sigh. "Okay."

Afraid she'd change her mind if he gave her time to think, he set his napkin on the table, picked up the receipt the server left after he paid the bill, and rose to pull out Rosalie's chair. She stood and looked up at him, then ran her tongue across lush lips that had lost all trace of lipstick.

He suppressed a moan and stepped back as he fought the urge to throw her down across the table and do unspeakably erotic things to her.

Instead, he took her arm like the gentleman he'd been raised to be, despite the jolt of lust down below when the mere touch of his hand on her bare skin made her gasp.

Rosalie fought to control her breath. The sparks set off by Morgan's hand on her arm lit tiny fires inside her.

Joey, she reminded herself. They'd hardly talked about him, or his future, over dinner. She needed to use this time with Morgan to get him to help her win custody.

He led her down a wooden staircase onto the beach. She stopped on the bottom step to slip off her sandals, shivering in the cool, damp wind that blew in the smell of salt and fish. Before she could stop him, he'd slid out of his jacket and put it across her shoulders, which enveloped her in the very different salt and tang of his body.

She shivered again, but not from cold. He put his arm around her waist while they walked down to the flat stretch of solid sand left behind by the tide. The moon left a trail of light across the water. To the south, the land and its lights curved out into the sea. To the north, the dark mass of the mountains showed only an isolated light here and there. Behind them sprawled a huge metropolis, but it felt as if they were all alone in the world on the moon-lit beach.

They walked north in a comfortable quiet after the pleasant intensity of their conversation over dinner. She tried once or twice to mention the custody battle, but the rhythmic rush of the waves lulled her into silence. Finally she let her thoughts scatter like the reflections on the ocean.

When they reached the edge of a private beach, Morgan stopped and turned her toward him to hold her in his arms.

She wasn't sure how she realized he meant to kiss her, but one moment they were two people who'd shared a pleasant conversation and the next moment the air between them had become an oven of desire and need, despite the fog creeping in around them.

She gave a tiny nod. He lowered his head slowly, as if afraid he might startle her. Unable to raise her arms to his shoulders because of the coat, she wrapped them around his waist and pulled him closer. His half-closed eyes sprang open and he smiled.

His lips touched hers and the world spun away. All that existed for her was the warmth where their lips touched, explored, nibbled, but still she smelled the sea and felt the damp sand under her feet. Flames swept down to her toes and settled in her breasts, low in her belly.

He slid his tongue across her lower lip, and she opened for him. She wanted more, too, wanted all of the delicious sensations he sent cascading through every barrier to free a person inside of her she'd forgotten existed.

She pushed up to her toes to be closer to the solid heat of his body. The brush of his hardness against her made her hesitate, test how it made her feel.

She almost laughed with surprise to find it made her feel sexy, powerful. She wiggled against it and he groaned.

How long they stood lost in each other, she couldn't have said. It might have been days, might easily have been all night. But after a while he pulled away, then nipped at her eyebrows, the line of her cheek, before he rested his forehead against hers and muttered a low oath that made her laugh in spite of herself.

She sank back to her heels, hands at his waist. He put his fingers on each side of her face and tipped it up to look at him.

"Rosalie?"

She closed her eyes, the spell of the kiss unbroken but now the colors behind her eyes were midnight blue instead of hazy purple.

"Rosalie, do you want to go back to my condo with me?"

Do you want to have sex with me? Her heart lurched. But the idea of ending this magical night now caused a pain deep inside her and overrode all caution.

This evening she'd learned Morgan was more than a man who reminded her what it meant to be a woman. He was a man she respected, liked, cared about. Which made it easier to admit she wanted the pleasure his kiss promised more than she'd ever wanted anything before.

One night. She owed herself one night.

She opened her eyes to find his still fixed on her face. She couldn't see love there, but she saw more than bare desire, so she whispered, "Yes."

He gave her a kiss so tender her heart nearly wept.

They strolled back in silence. She heard the crash and sweep of the waves, each thunderous beat of her heart, maybe the beat of his. But her hand in his felt right, the occasional bump of their hips as they walked a rhythm she recognized from some ancient dream.

Once they reached the wooden stairway back up to the restaurant, he steadied her with his hand while she brushed sand off her feet and slipped on her sandals. When he released her hand to brush the sand from his elegant shoes she suppressed a whimper of need.

She stood in the circle of his arms to wait for the valet to bring the car. When Morgan slipped his jacket from her shoulders before she climbed in, she shivered with more than cold.

The thunk of the door the valet closed behind her had a ring of erotic inevitability that tingled through her body and made her heart sing.

Morgan pulled onto Pacific Coast Highway, his mind almost as troubled as his body was aroused. This plan had to work. If it didn't, Lillian might get custody of Joey.

Worse, Charlie's father could still decide his latest wife's youth might play well in court if Lillian was the alternative and sue for custody after all. Morgan had tried to persuade him he didn't have much chance, but Paul Thompson never backed down from a fight.

Maybe the best idea was to explain it all and lay out his plan to Rosalie, make the case to her directly. That's what he'd planned to do when he asked her to dinner.

But Morgan knew her better now. Logic alone would never break through the walls of distrust she'd built around herself when it came to men.

He needed to engage her emotions, her passion, if his plan was to have any chance of success. His passion was already plenty engaged. And he'd enjoyed their conversation over dinner enough that someday his emotions might come into the equation too, once he was sure she couldn't walk away from him the way his mother had.

Rosalie began to tense up, maybe change her mind.

The seats in the damned hybrid were too far apart for him to put his arm around her, so he clicked on the sound system to distract her.

He was in luck. Mozart danced out of the speakers, light and airy, with a subtle sexual undercurrent. From the corner of his eye he saw her smile as she loosened her hold on her shawl and sank back into the comfort of the leather seat.

"How come you're such a classical music fan?" he asked.

"It's what I grew up with. Mother always painted to it. By the time I was old enough to be exposed to the music other kids listened to, it seemed flat and way too simple to me."

"I bet the other kids loved it when you told them that."

She gave a low laugh. "I wasn't very popular, anyway. Everyone was too busy pitying me because my mom was sick to be my friend."

"Everyone knew, even in a big city like L.A.?"

"I went to the local school and my mom was very active in the parent-teacher organization. I guess you went to private schools, huh?"

Private schools, where they were only allowed to listen to classical music. Schools where it took lots of As and good behavior to convince the teachers he wasn't like his step-brother. Most of the kids never got past the stories they'd heard about Charlie Thompson. And some of them got a thrill out of bullying the kid brother of the school's most notorious bully.

He put his hand on Rosalie's knee, half to erase the memories, half to comfort her, but the feel of her skin pushed the heat out of the comfort zone and into lust.

She didn't shy away from his touch, as he might have expected, but gave a soft gasp instead and shifted her body toward him in a probably unintended invitation.

A horn honked. He was stopped in the middle of Sunset Boulevard with a green light overhead. Cars swooshed past him on both sides.

So much for his attempt to multitask his plan, sex and driving. He pulled his hand away and refocused on the traffic around him.

Rosalie had let herself sink too deeply into the music. She sat up with a start when Morgan drove into an underground garage and switched off the engine.

Contentment became excitement in a heartbeat. Tiny flashes of anticipation battled with more familiar clouds of doubt while she waited for him to open the car door for her.

Then her hand was in his. He smiled at her with such an intense look her insides leapt into flame. She was out of the car and in his arms before she was aware she'd moved.

He claimed her mouth with impressive expertise, her arms around his neck, her hands buried in the thick, black hair that curled around the collar of his jacket.

The night, the wine, the conversation had filled her with a need, a hope she couldn't deny.

He must have nudged the door, because it fell shut. She leaned back against the car, her breasts hot with need and raised into his chest.

He took her face in his hands and deepened the kiss, plundered and teased her mouth until she moaned. Her arms dropped to his waist to draw his hardness tighter against her. He shifted closer still and ran his hands slowly down her neck, her shoulders . . .

Her whole body trembled when he caressed the sides of her breasts. The lace bra, already pulled tight against her nipples, teased them now in a heady pleasure-pain. She rubbed against the warm wall of his flesh, so close and yet still not close enough.

He groaned and rocked against the vee of her thighs. His thumbs reached out to caress her hard nipples.

All the desire she'd bottled up since she met him spilled out and transported her to the first moment she'd looked into his eyes and knew he was all she'd ever dreamed of in a man.

His hands dropped to her thighs to tug up the full skirt of her dress. She lifted her hips from the side of the car in a wanton invitation that made her want to laugh with joy.

Morgan had both hands fisted in Rosalie's skirt before he remembered she wasn't the kind of woman to have rough sex shoved up against a car.

She seemed fine with it, more than fine with it right now, but as soon as it was over he suspected she'd regret it. And regret was not what he wanted her to feel.

Her tiny gasp when he let her skirt drop echoed his body's more vehement protest. He hesitated, but the image of the shame on her face after the lust wore off gave him the strength to put some space between them. He dropped kisses of regret on her face while he eased away.

"We need to take this upstairs," he whispered.

She blinked owlishly, like a child awakened from a dream, which made him chuckle and kiss the corner of each eye.

Before either of them spoke, the metallic growl of the garage door opening echoed off the concrete walls around them.

Rosalie's eyes went wide and a rosy flush crept up her cheeks.

"I guess I sort of lost track of where we were." She looked away

He tipped her chin up with one finger and gave her a quick kiss. "We both did."

He held his breath. Now her head was clearer, there was always the chance she'd change her mind.

Instead, she took his hand in hers, which immediately rekindled the banked fires inside him. He kissed her hand before he tucked it under his arm and led her to the elevator.

The whisper of the elevator doors closing behind them sent alarms bells off in Rosalie's head. But the moment she tensed, before the thought of changing her mind could even form itself, Morgan swept her up in his arms again for a kiss as sweet as it was passionate. The sound of the alarm bells melted into the Mozart they'd listened to in the car.

One night. One night to make up for the boyfriend who wanted her to put her mother in a "home," sell the house, put the money in a joint account, and move in with him. To make up for the law students who lost interest in her because she had the top grades in her class. To make up for grown men too focused on their pleasure, their needs. One night for her.

When the elevator doors opened again, he released her and crossed the private foyer to unlock the double door.

"Why do you own a condo in L.A.?" she asked in the almost palatial quiet despite the busy city far below.

"I don't. My company does. It's a first move toward a second office here, for better access to the Asian markets. That's another reason the L.A. start-up is attractive to us."

He opened the door and Rosalie stepped through, stunned into silence. The sheer opulence of the condo was beyond anything she'd ever seen before.

When she stepped into the huge leather, glass and chrome living room, her feet sank into the carpet. Fresh roses scented the air. Floor-to-ceiling windows filled one wall.

The penthouse condo sat atop the canyon of condos and luxury office buildings along Wilshire Boulevard, so the city lights spread far below them were like gems on black velvet.

Morgan pushed a button and the curtains swung closed. She was about to protest when she saw the painting over the fireplace.

"A Martha Ritchard." The huge canvas was painted with thick

slashes of vibrant color on black. The sheer emotional impact of it staggered her. "She was one of my mother's teachers."

"I'm not surprised to hear that."

Morgan slid his coat off and loosed his tie. He looked uncomfortable, as if he didn't know what to do or say next. Unlikely, given he must have had dozens of women up here before. Still, the touch of awkwardness made her smile. And made her brave. She dropped her shawl next to his jacket on the back of the gray-leather sofa and walked over to him.

He swallowed. "Would you like a drink?"

"No." She lifted her hands to his shoulders and raised her lips to his.

He hesitated a moment before he wrapped his arms around her and turned her simple kiss into a lesson in sensual expertise.

Her whole body shivered with need the moment he plunged his tongue into her already-sensitized mouth. Ruthlessly he plundered, tasted, possessed, but the need only grew deeper.

He withdrew part way and she followed, half to quiet the alarm bells in her mind, half to ignite the same fires inside him that threatened to consume her as she stood there, fully dressed.

But not for long. He ended the kiss gently, his hands still on the nape of her neck to caress and tease them both as he stepped away.

"Are you sure?" His voice was rough, his jaw tight.

She dropped her gaze from the intensity in his. "Yes."

His posture softened and he grinned

"Good, because those buttons have driven me crazy all night."

He drew his hands from her neck to trail fire down her shoulders and along the top of her dress until his fingers reached the first button.

When he bent his head to lick the rounded flesh above the cloth, she stifled a gasp that shivered through her body in little bursts of delight.

*

Morgan took another deep breath to calm the almost unbearable need to rip those buttons apart and fill himself with the sight, the feel, the taste of the breasts he'd daydreamed about since the first day he walked into Rosalie's office. But a quick roll on the couch wasn't her style any more than rough sex in the garage. She needed, she deserved, tenderness.

He undid the first button and spread the fabric it released. He lifted his hands away, and she let out a long, slow breath, then gasped in more air when he repeated the process with the second button.

He'd expected to find white, boring cotton under the blue of her dress. A bra Joey's mother would wear. The silky blue lace he'd revealed brought a new burst of lust that made him grit his teeth against the increased pressure down below.

She hadn't dressed like Joey's mother. She'd dressed like a woman who wanted to have sex with him.

He smiled and rewarded her with a kiss just below her ear. She sighed and pressed her body toward him in encouragement.

He didn't need to be reminded twice. The next two buttons went quickly, despite the tremor in his hands.

He spread the fabric open again to reveal two hard, pink nipples behind the blue lace, their eagerness so obvious he couldn't resist the urge to catch each one between a thumb and finger.

Rosalie stopped breathing again while he decided between a tweak and a tug. In the end, he did both. The air swooshed out of her in the tiniest of moans. His body tightened another uncomfortable notch, but he turned his attention back to the buttons and the remaining treasure they concealed.

Three more and he'd be able to slide the straps of the dress off her shoulders.

A faint flush rose on the creamy skin. Reverently he raised his hands to her breasts, the way she leaned into his touch as much an enticement as the soft flesh itself. He caressed, weighed, tweaked and tugged again at her engorged nipples until she trembled and pulled away.

He made short work of undoing the remaining buttons. When he dropped his hands, she stepped away to let the dress billow to the floor around her feet. Her eyes were green pools of wonder and desire. Along with a tinge of the wariness that made her the woman she was.

But, to his surprise and delight, she blinked the wariness away, slid out of her slip, reached behind her and dropped her bra to the floor beside it.

"Maybe we should take this to the bedroom." His voice was rough with desire.

She hesitated a moment before she nodded and held out her hand.

To touch only her quivering fingers with all of her lush body within his reach was exquisite torture, but he led her down the short hall to the bedroom, kissed her palm before he released her hand, and pulled down the duvet.

She stared a moment at the bed, then turned to him.

"You're overdressed." Her voice was a thin thread of sound, as if she hadn't taken a full breath since they stepped off the elevator.

"So I am," he said in mock surprise. "Do you want to do the honors?"

She pursed her lips. "I'd rather watch."

This woman with her unique blend of shy and brazen would be the death of him.

Self-consciously he took off his shirt, shoes and socks, but faltered with his hands at the buckle of his belt.

She'd sat on the edge of the bed, her legs tucked together and her hands at her sides to hold her up.

She looked up at his eyes when he stopped and licked her lips.

The rest of his clothes fell away as if of their own accord and he walked to the bed, his swollen flesh inches from her sweet mouth.

She touched his hardness with one hesitant finger. "I never . . ."

His control snapped. He tumbled her on the bed and feasted on those creamy breasts, those sweet-as-berries lips, and the nectar of her mouth. Her little sighs, the way her hands stroked his shoulders, his back, his butt, fed his hunger for her.

He returned to the rose-bud nipples to lick and suck until she moaned and gave a tiny shudder of delight. Damn but this woman was hot. All he'd ever dreamed of—and more.

He eased back to take his time, despite the urgency gnawing at him. He let his hands explore the secrets of her body, find where his touch made her tremble, where it made her gasp, where it made her moan again.

He marked her with every kiss, every nibble, until she was his completely.

Which should have frightened him to death.

A cloud of fear hovered beyond the dizzying pleasure that had taken possession of Rosalie's body. Not physical fear. She'd trust Morgan with her life. But she'd never trust any man with her heart.

Still, she let him take control of her every sensation without a second thought. She owed herself the pleasure he could give her, just this once.

She squirmed with erotic eagerness as his kisses and caresses made her senses dance. Her body became pure need under his gentle fingers, his hot mouth, those perfect teeth that knew exactly how to use a gentle nip to send her into new spirals of ecstasy.

His hand found the center of her need and slowed the caresses to pay minute attention to her every breath of desire. The effort it must have cost him made her smile until all reason slipped away.

She was already on the verge of ecstasy when he slid down her body and used his clever tongue to tease and sample and drive her wild, every muscle tight.

He suckled the exquisitely tender flesh until she gave a low wail, then she crashed over the edge with a single word. "Now!"

He moved away, but before she could protest she heard the tear of foil, and her heart filled with warmth.

He'd remembered to protect her from her own mindless need for him.

Then he was on her, in her, and time stopped, circled, spun with the ancient dance. The frenzy of pleasure grew hotter, sweeter until he made a low, questioning sound and she lifted her hips in eager response.

He raised up on his knees, grasped her hips and plunged home one last time. Her pleasure echoed his as they soared high into the midnight-blue sky and sank together back into the silken darkness.

A quiver of delight brought Rosalie back to reality some time later, with the dim awareness it was not the first aftershock to what had been the best sex of her life. She let the words echo through her brain, surprised to find they seemed to belong there, as if good sex was part of her, not something she might find time for someday.

Sensations drifted through her muddled mind. The sleekness of silk sheets. The warmth of the duvet. The heat of the hard male body next to her. Shock reverberated through her.

She'd done the deed with Morgan Danby!

He protested sleepily when she jerked to a sitting position, the duvet wrapped around her.

She glanced around the room. If she could get dressed and sneak . . .

Her clothes weren't in this room. Just the tiny scrap of blue lace he'd pulled off her body . . .

Or did she pull off her panties? She wasn't sure. Shame washed over her.

No, not shame. Embarrassment. Shame would mean she was sorry for what happened, but to her surprise, she wasn't sorry at all.

She was still trying to sort out her tumbled emotions when a muscular arm wrapped itself around her waist and tried to tug her gently back down toward the undertow. It slid away at her resistance. Morgan raised a sleepy head to frown up at her.

"Regrets?"

She felt her face go hot, but she owed the man honesty. "No. Just . . ."

He sat beside her, the duvet across his lap. "Not sure?"

"Closer."

The air turned thick, not with the sexual heat from before, but with unruly thoughts, unsaid words. She didn't have much experience with situations like this, and none with men like Morgan.

He stared at the painting on the wall across from them—another Ritchard, maybe a nude, but she wasn't sure—as the minutes stretched out between them.

"Rosalie?"

The tone of his voice, the way he didn't look at her, made her heart race. Was he the one with regrets? Was he eager to get rid of her?

Or did he want to tell her he loved her?

He cleared his throat. "Rosalie?" he asked again.

She held her breath.

"Will you marry me?"

Her mind went blank. "What?"

"Will you marry me?"

"Are you crazy?" She couldn't suppress a laugh—half genuine surprise, half unexpected disappointment that cut her in two.

The sound froze his face into the mask she remembered too

well from the day they'd first met. The memories crashed through her post-orgasmic haze.

Please, she urged silently, don't let this be about Joey.

"It makes perfect sense," Morgan said. "You love Joey."

And I almost fell in love with you, you almighty jerk! But no way would she ever let him know. She wrapped her arms around herself, suddenly cold inside.

"If you marry me," he went on in a much-too-reasonable tone, "we'd be able to adopt Joey together and Lillian can see him whenever she wants."

"All this," she waved one arm at the rumpled bed, "to make Charlie's mother happy?"

"No. It was to make you happy. I don't want you to lose Joey."

"I can fight my own battles, thank you." Her voice quavered. "Why not just tell me what you had in mind? Why pretend you liked me? Why have sex with me?"

"I do like you. I wanted you to feel safe with me."

Outrage burned away the threat of tears. "Safe with you! So you could manipulate me better? What kind of safety is that?"

"Think for a minute. If you marry me, everyone can get what they want. Lillian gets her grandson. You get to keep Joey."

"And what do you get?"

Chapter Nine

Morgan already knew he'd blown it, but Rosalie's question had sent a new shock wave through him.

"I get a wife." For the first time in his life, he found no other words for how he felt, what he wanted from a woman.

"For how long?"

Forever.

Nothing is forever. Not even a mother's love.

"Until one of us wants out," he said instead

"Not good enough."

"Maybe bed isn't the best place to discuss this. Why don't you shower and get dressed while I make coffee?" It'd be easier to focus on winning her over without her warm, naked body next to him. "I have a plan. You'll see it's the best solution all the way around."

"If I listen to your plan, will you go away and leave me and Joey alone? For good?"

Reluctantly, he nodded. One chance was better than none.

Not that he could stay away from her, not after tonight. He closed his eyes, remembering the heat of her mouth, the way her body melted into his, the gasps of pleasure he'd coaxed from her.

As she'd once said, he liked to win. And he knew of no battle more important to win than this one.

Rosalie waited until Morgan left the room before she crept out of the bed. The opulent marble and chrome of the en-suite bathroom was wasted on her as she tried to scrub away the memories of what she'd done in the hot flow of the shower.

The clash between the warm water and the arctic chill inside dizzied her. Each beat of her heart, each breath, was an effort. She felt like Lucifer, plunged from the heights of heaven to the icy depths, but couldn't for the life of her figure out what she'd done to deserve it.

But wasn't that the lesson she'd learned from her mother's illness? Things happen. What we deserve doesn't come into it. All you can do is make the best of what life gives you.

And what was the best to be made of the fiasco of having sex with Morgan Danby?

She found her clothes laid on the bed when she came out of the bathroom. She dressed with hands that shook so much she was barely able to do up the buttons Morgan had undone so easily.

"So tell me this wonderful plan you have," she found the courage to ask once she was seated across from him at the marble breakfast bar where he'd place two mugs of coffee. "If I were crazy enough to marry you, we'd adopt Joey, but then what? Where would we live?"

He frowned. "In Boston."

She raised her eyebrows.

"There's a nice, big two-bedroom loft for sale in my condo building."

The hot coffee did little to melt the ice inside of her, but the bitter taste seemed right and the caffeine supplied false energy to let her play his game for a while.

"A loft? With no real walls, low window sills, and an open stairway?"

He gave a glum nod.

"Does it have a yard?"

Clearly something he hadn't thought of.

"It has a balcony."

She shook her head in disbelief.

He blinked twice and tried again. "The building is close to the Commons. You could take Joey to the playground there every day."

"But what would I do for work? I'm not a member of the Massachusetts bar, and taking a second bar exam at this point in my life does not sound like fun."

"You'll take care of Joey. Isn't that what you've wanted to do all along?"

"I want to be his mother, but I'm a lawyer, not a nanny."

Morgan stiffened and took a sip of his coffee.

"I don't want Joey to be raised by someone who cares more about their paycheck than they do about him."

She started to tell him how wonderful the workers at Joey's day-care center were, but the expression on Morgan's face told her his words had less to do with Joey and more to do with his own past.

For a moment the ice around her heart cracked enough for her wonder what it must have been like to be Charlie's little brother—or worse, his stepbrother—when all the servants worked for Charlie's mother. Then she remembered what had happened between them and decided to save her sympathy for someone who deserved it.

"I'm supposed to sacrifice my career, my home, my life to move to Boston and be an unpaid nanny for Joey? Why would I, why would anyone do that? On the off-chance that his grand-mother can win a custody suit?"

When Morgan didn't respond, she steamed on ahead.

"If I do agree to this insane scheme, how long do you plan on staying married? You said until one of us wants out, but what does that mean? Until Joey starts school? Until he goes away to boarding school?" She didn't hide her contempt for the idea. "Until he goes to college? And what happens after the divorce?"

"Whoa! You're getting way ahead of yourself. I don't foresee a set end date for our marriage."

But he did foresee an end date. No doubt right when she needed him most.

"If we do, did divorce, you'd get a settlement large enough to let you live wherever and however you please. Go back to L.A., if you want. You'd never need to work again."

"Did it occur to you that I might want to work, that I might like what I do?" She tapped one fingernail on the marble surface between them. "Tell me again how giving up everything I've accomplished in my life makes sense from my point of view."

He didn't know much about women, Morgan realized, as he searched for the words to answer her. Sure, he knew what to do in bed to keep them happy and eager for more. And he

knew how to charm them if it suited his purposes, and how to shut the charm off if it didn't. But he'd never let a woman get close enough for him to learn how to get his way with her once she saw through the charm. No woman had gotten that far, or wanted to, until Rosalie.

His life had been a series of one-night stands, even if the same woman was involved. He'd never spent a whole night with a woman, unless he counted the time in high school he and his date had fallen asleep in the back seat of her father's Rover. Or nights the sex lasted until dawn.

Thinking about sex while he tried to make Rosalie see reason was a bad idea. It made him notice how she rubbed her fingers up and down the side of her mug, how the scent of his soap became flowery and feminine on her skin. It reminded him of the bliss they'd shared.

"I'm a very rich man," he was horrified to hear himself say.

She gave him a look that would have frozen stone.

Unable to help himself, he reached out to lay his hand on her arm, to make her stay. Her skin seared him, but her eyes froze him out. The softness of her flesh was too much to resist. He rubbed his hand slowly down her arm to her hand, and smiled to himself when she didn't pull away. He lifted her hand to his mouth and kissed the palm.

"And, as you know, a very good lover."

She blinked, as if waking from a dream, jerked her hand away and stood up in a single, almost violent, motion.

"Goodbye, Morgan Danby. I do not have to damn you to hell. I'm quite sure you can get there all on your own."

To Rosalie's shock, a look that might have been genuine pain, crossed Morgan's face, quickly replaced by the familiar stony mask.

"At least let me drive you home."

"You *are* home," she pointed out. "But you can call me a cab."

He did. He also rode the elevator with her down to the building's lobby and waited with her until the cab appeared. He handed the driver some money and gave him the address while the doorman helped her into the cab. Then the man who'd made such wonderful love to her, the man who'd asked her to marry him, turned and walked inside without a backward glance.

She nursed her anger all the way through the long cab ride home. The effort exhausted her enough that she was able to sleep once she got there.

The next day she continued the litany of reasons why Morgan Danby was a diabolical jerk and not worth even one minute of her attention.

Still, when Vanessa came by the office that afternoon to ask how the date had gone, Rosalie found she couldn't tell her friend what had happened. She muttered platitudes about the great dinner, but said Morgan wasn't her type.

"How can a rich, smart, charming, handsome man not be your type?"

"He's arrogant and has to have him own way."

"You mean he didn't let you control the situation?"

Rosalie's jaw dropped. "I'm not . . . I don't . . ."

"You don't need to be in control?" Vanessa swung her hand around the meticulously neat office. "I don't blame you, given how out of control your mother's health was, but someday you need to grow up and learn out-of-control isn't always bad."

Rosalie closed her eyes, surprised when a tear rolled down her face.

Vanessa swore under her breath. "What happened last night, Rosalie? Did he hurt you? Should I send Aaron after him?"

"No. I'm fine. I'm tired. We were out late."

Before her friend could ask more painful questions, the receptionist called in to say Vanessa's next appointment was there. She stood and gave Rosalie a worried look.

"You decide you want to talk about it, you know where to find me."

Alone again, Rosalie took deep breaths to clear her mind. But despite her best efforts it filled again with memories of the night before. She should have been furious with Morgan. She *was* furious with him. But the anger was mixed with a sadness she hadn't expected.

Sadness that she'd never have such great sex again, she told herself, but it didn't stick.

Sadness, she had to admit, that she'd never see Morgan again. She liked the man, dammit. Or the man she'd thought he was. Her devotion to the truth eventually forced her to admit she more than liked him. That was the worst of it, what carved an aching hollow in her chest.

So the real sadness was at the death of another illusion. The illusion of a cure for her mother. The illusion her father would come back to them. The illusion she'd ever be able to count on anyone besides herself.

She didn't sleep well that night. Her dreams were too full of the good parts of her evening with Morgan. And those parts had been very, very good.

In the dark hours before dawn, she awoke to the memory of the moment he'd touched her after she froze up when he mentioned how rich he was. He'd put his hand on her arm as if he couldn't bear for her to leave. For an instant, she realized, with a new ache in her chest, she'd seen the face of a boy whose mother had walked out on him.

Rosalie didn't sleep well for the next week either, but she'd been through worse. Time would take away the lingering heartache from the—what? certainly not relationship—fiasco with Morgan Danby. In the meantime, she had Joey, her work, and her friends to get her through.

She was putting the files she needed to work on over the weekend into her laptop bag the next Friday evening when her office phone rang. Despite the late hour, she picked it up. She needed every client she could get with a custody battle to finance.

"Ms. Rosalie Walker?" The efficient female voice sounded like a secretary.

Rosalie's foolish heart jumped to her throat and froze there. "Yes?"

A click, then a moment of silence. Rosalie forced a breath past the tightness in her throat.

"Ms. Walker?" Another woman's voice.

Rosalie's heart plummeted past its usual place and deep into her belly. "Yes?"

"This is Lillian Danby, Charleston Thompson's mother. I want to see my grandson."

Rosalie hovered between mother and lawyer.

To buy the time to think, she asked, "Are you in Los Angeles?"

"Yes," the other woman huffed. "Where else would I be?"

Rosalie suppressed a rude suggestion or two before she let the lawyer take over.

"You have no legal visitation rights at this time."

"My attorney says, since the DNA evidence proves I'm the baby's grandmother, I do have some rights."

"Strictly speaking, a court would have to order an unwilling custodial parent or guardian to grant you those rights."

And strictly speaking, Joey wasn't a baby anymore, but Rosalie let it pass.

A noise that sounded like a sob came over the phone. "How can you be so cruel? I just want to see my grandchild."

Rosalie wished she could call Joey's social worker to ask what would be best for him, but a quick glance at the time told her Ms. Cameron would have already left the office for the weekend. It was too late to call the lawyer Rosalie had consulted about the adoption and possible custody case, too. She closed her eyes and tried to figure out what she'd advise a client who was in a situation like this.

"Are you still there?" Mrs. Danby asked. "You didn't hang up on me, did you?"

"No. I'm trying to decide what's best for Joey."

"What's best is for him to be with his grandmother. I'm all the family he has left, the poor baby."

Yes, and why is that? Rosalie managed not to ask. Mrs. Danby didn't seem the type to accept any responsibility for Charlie's actions. Maybe she wasn't responsible, but all this might have been easier if Rosalie had been able to believe the woman ever considered the possibility.

Another sob-like sound brought her mind back to the advice she'd give someone else.

"I could bring him to a public place to meet you."

"I want you to bring him to my hotel room." Mrs. Danby's voice held no hint of tears. "I'm sure to fall apart when I see the little dear, and I hate to cry in public. My makeup runs."

Rosalie shook her head as she imagined Joey's reaction to a weepy stranger who wanted to cuddle him, but his grandmother seemed to have no idea what toddlers were like.

"I'm sorry. It has to be a public place. Perhaps the lobby of your hotel or a restaurant?"

Mrs. Danby sniffed. "The hotel doesn't have a restaurant."

An exclusive boutique hotel, no doubt. "Where are you staying?"

"Santa Monica. The room has a nice view of the ocean I'm sure little Joey would enjoy."

Yeah, right. Little kids loved to sit still and look at the view. What planet was this woman from? Oh, yes, Planet Nanny.

"We can meet at Santa Monica Place," Rosalie suggested. "It's a mall near the ocean."

"A shopping mall?" Mrs. Danby sounded horrified.

Rosalie rubbed her forehead. Somehow she'd acquired a stereotypical mother-in-law without a husband. She turned to her computer and found the Santa Monica city website.

"There's a big pedestrian promenade next to the mall. We can meet at the north end, near Santa Monica Boulevard."

"I suppose that will do. What time tonight?"

"Not tonight. It's better if I bring him to meet you tomorrow morning when he won't be so tired." And I'll have more energy to deal with you. "What about nine o'clock?"

"In the morning?" Mrs. Danby gasped. "Let's say eleven. I need time to prepare myself."

Rosalie rolled her eyes. "Eleven will be fine."

"We'll see you then. Goodbye."

Before Rosalie could find the breath to ask what "we" meant, the other woman clicked off.

Morgan considered himself lucky he'd been able to convince Lillian not to call a cab for the three-block walk from her hotel to where they were supposed to meet Rosalie and Joey.

Now he'd have to rely on more good luck if he wanted to make Plan B work, after the way he'd botched Plan A.

A moment's thought would have told him, if there were two

things Rosalie didn't want a man to offer her, money and great sex would head the list. Not that she wasn't open to great sex, but that's not what she'd want to hear. Not first, or second. If the old-fashioned phrase "not that kind of woman" ever applied to anyone, it applied to Rosalie Walker.

The problem was, he hadn't thought at all. He'd reacted in a moment of blind panic and tried any way he could to keep her from walking away.

The last time his whole life seemed to depend on stopping a woman from walking away, he'd refused to kiss his mother goodbye. That hadn't worked so well, either.

"Is that them?" Lillian asked. "Morgan, I'm shaking."

She held out a carefully manicured hand that did, indeed, quiver. Real emotion from Lillian. Who would have expected it?

He steeled himself, then followed Lillian's gaze to the bench where Rosalie sat with Joey in her lap, reading him a book.

She looked as if she hadn't been sleeping well, but that might have been wishful thinking based on his own recent familiarity with guilt and regret-induced insomnia.

In any case, she was dressed to impress. Somewhere she'd acquired enough knowledge of women like Lillian to find the perfect medium between the lawyer Rosalie and the mother Rosalie. Her dark hair was piled up on her head and she wore pearl earrings that matched the necklace visible at the neckline of her blue silk blouse. Tailored slacks showed off her curves, and pink toes peeked out at him from her low-heeled sandals.

His insides twisted.

As they walked closer, he realized she'd dressed Joey up, too. The kid wore red corduroy pull-up pants instead of his usual jeans, and a woven shirt with matching stripes instead of the usual t-shirt. He'd already wiggled enough to undo one of the buttons across his belly and reveal a slash of pink baby flesh.

When Rosalie saw them, her Joey-smile faded, replaced by

something like panic. She recovered quickly, stowed the book in the tote next to her, and stood up with Joey on one hip.

Rosalie felt all the wind rush out of her in a whoosh.

She'd half expected Morgan to show up with his stepmother, but the reality carried a wallop ten times more powerful than the thought.

She refocused on the woman at his side. She'd often wondered what kind of woman could have raised Charlie, but she would never have come up with anyone like Lillian Danby.

The first thing she noticed was the older woman's apparent fragility. She was very slender, the hand on Morgan's arm almost a claw, her legs shapely but so thin Rosalie wondered how she found stockings to fit. The woman's face was thin too, and had the rigidity of repeated cosmetic surgery. What was the saying? "You can never be too thin or too rich."

Mrs. Danby wore a black designer skirt, cream-colored blouse, and a bright-red jacket that should have been too warm on such a sunny day, but her eyes were the same watery blue as Charlie's and, like his, hard as diamonds. Behind the fragile façade, Rosalie saw the unbending will of someone who'd heard the word "no" too little when she was a child, and was rich enough to ignore it now she was an adult. Oh, yes, this was Charlie's mother.

"How do you do?"

Mrs. Danby ignored her proffered hand, eyes fixed on Joey.

"You lied to me, Morgan. He doesn't look at all like my poor Charleston."

When the strange lady brushed one hand across Joey's cheek, he jerked his head away and buried it in Rosalie's shoulder.

"He has the same round face as that woman. And her little nose. The men in my family all had substantial noses."

And the women all had their noses fixed, Rosalie suspected.

"He's a toddler," Morgan said. "Who knows what he'll look like later on?"

Was that the best he could do? Rosalie shot him a glare, but he turned away with a shrug.

Mrs. Danby belatedly held out her hand. "You must be Ms. Walker, the woman who's been taking care of my grandson."

"I'm his guardian, yes."

Mrs. Danby's handshake was surprisingly firm and brief enough to border on rudeness. An awkward silence fell amid the bustle of the plaza around them.

"Why don't you introduce Joey to his grandmother?" Morgan suggested.

At the sound of his name, Joey stared up sideways at the tall man next to the strange woman and muttered, "Mawg," as if he too, was surprised at his step-uncle's pandering behavior.

She's the only family I have, Morgan had told her.

But Joey was the only family Rosalie had.

"Why don't we sit down?" she suggested.

She sank back down on the bench, arms tired from holding Joey so tightly. Luckily he settled on her lap without protest.

Mrs. Danby frowned at the bench, probably afraid it carried some dire contamination, raised her eyes skyward, then sat primly next to Rosalie. That left the far end of the bench for Morgan, out of Rosalie's range of sight.

"Joey," she coaxed, "this is your grandmother." She turned to Mrs. Danby with a forced smile. "What do you want him to call you? Grandmother is quite a mouthful at his age."

Horror dawned on the other woman's face. "Grandmother? No. Maybe . . . maybe Nana? That doesn't sound so old, does it?"

This last question was to Morgan, who responded with a small grunt.

"Joey, this is Nana. Mrs. Danby, this is Joey."

A moment too late Rosalie remembered "nana" was Joey's word for bananas. He looked around for the promised snack and ignored the woman who had leaned in to kiss him.

"No nana."

Mrs. Danby pulled back. "You've already taught him to hate me, haven't you? I knew I should have demanded custody as soon as Morgan found my little darling."

"Not that it would have been legally possible," Morgan commented from the other end of the bench.

Rosalie took a deep breath for patience, not sure which of them she hated more.

"No," she corrected. "Joey thinks I promised him a banana. Maybe we should find another name for him to call you."

Mrs. Danby relaxed her rigid posture a little. "He could call me Lillian. That's what his father always called me."

Rosalie wasn't sure how far to trust the glint of moisture in the other woman's eyes, but tried again with Joey.

"Honey, this is Lillian. Can you say 'Lillian'?"

"Lin." Joey touched Mrs. Danby's face. "Lin."

"He's adorable, isn't he?" The older woman was talking to Morgan again, as if Rosalie wasn't there, or as if she was a servant. "I'm sure he knows who I am."

"Do you want to hold him?" Rosalie offered reluctantly.

Horror returned to Mrs. Danby's face. "His face is so . . . damp. See, he left a mark on your blouse. I can't go around with wet spots on my clothes. What would people think?"

Rosalie didn't even want to count all the ways that response was wrong. "So, what do you want to do now?"

"I'd like to take the little dear back to my hotel with me."

"No," both Rosalie and Morgan said at the same time.

Morgan's body had gone tense. Was he there to stop his step-mother physically, if necessary, or to help her take Joey away from her?

Cold prickles ran up Rosalie's spine. She pulled the child away from his grandmother and held him so tightly he gave a grunt of protest.

No. Reason pushed away panic. These two people were not

about to commit a federal crime by kidnapping Joey on a crowded plaza. She forced herself to take long, slow breaths.

"Perhaps this had been enough of a visit for today." She took the ice of her panic and put it into her voice.

"Perhaps so." Morgan stood up and took his stepmother's arm.

She stood. A tear trickled down her cheek.

"How can you be so heartless?"

Since it wasn't clear which of them she'd spoken to, Rosalie chose to ignore the accusation.

Morgan shot Rosalie an apologetic look. "Lillian, that's enough. I don't know what you meant to accomplish by demanding to see Joey, but you've done it now. Let's leave Ms. Walker and her son in peace."

Mrs. Danby directed an ineffectual slap at his chest. "He is not her son. He's mine. My grandchild. I can't leave him here with her."

"Yes, you can, and you will," Morgan replied. "Right now."

His tone, like his body, was so tight with rigidly controlled anger that Joey burst into tears.

"See, he doesn't want me to go."

"Or he wants you to go. Hard to tell. Rosalie . . ."

The way he said her name made her knees feel so weak she was glad she was already sitting down. Damn his eyes.

"Rosalie, why don't you take him away and see how he reacts?"

Past ready for the ordeal to be over she shifted Joey to hold him with one arm while she gathered their things with her free hand and dumped them in the stroller. She pulled herself to her feet, Joey and all, and started the stroller toward where she'd parked the car.

Joey stopped crying. Over her shoulder he called "Bye, Mawg."

A burst of pride lightened her steps, despite the awkward scene behind them. Two two-word sentences in one day!

She pushed the stroller faster, eager to get as far as possible from both the Danbys.

"That was cruel, Morgan," Lillian told him as they watched Rosalie walk away. "How can you let her take my grandson?"

"She isn't taking him, she's keeping him. For good, if I have anything to say about it."

"You don't," his stepmother barked, but then seemed to sag under the weight of the encounter with Joey. "I refuse to walk all the way back to my hotel. Find me a cab."

He looked over his shoulder for Rosalie. She was headed toward the mall.

Luckily two taxis were parked at the near end of the plaza. He helped Lillian into one of them, gave the driver a twenty and the name of her hotel, then rushed after Rosalie over his stepmother's protests.

The plaza was full of women with strollers, but only one of them drew him toward her like a magnet. She'd stopped by another bench and sat down to clear the gear out of the stroller so she could put Joey in it, but the wriggly toddler had other ideas.

"Here we go, buddy," Morgan said as he scooped Joey from her arms.

She gave him a glare that would send a lesser man into full retreat.

"How about you go to you-know-where and take your stepmother with you?"

He sat beside her and bounced Joey up and down his knee.

"Hey, I had nothing to do with it. I found out she was here when she called me from her hotel yesterday. All I could do was damage control."

"Because you happened to be in Los Angeles yet again?"

Chapter Ten

Morgan shifted his grip on the kid so he didn't have to look at her. He'd used the last week to pull strings and make deals to ensure Paul Thompson would never sue for custody of Joey again. Once he'd won that battle, he'd caught the next flight out here to see if he could find a way to make Rosalie understand that, as clumsy and ill-timed as his bedside proposal had been, God help him, he actually did want to marry her. He'd figured he'd tell her about Thompson, then get them past the fiasco of last weekend and back on track with his plan, which now was as much about the two of them as about Joey.

Until Lillian dropped her little stink bomb in his path.

The wave of anger distracted him enough that he loosened his hold on Joey. The kid broke free and toddled off at full speed toward the cheerful music of a mariachi band.

Morgan and Rosalie both lunged after Joey, bumped into each other, and tumbled to the pavement. Somehow he managed to land on the bottom, one arm around her, his other flung out to break their fall.

She gave a quiet "Oof" when they landed.

For a long moment they stared at each other, the air between them hot with pent-up need.

Dimly he heard Joey screech and a man's voice say, "This your kid?"

Rosalie scrambled up off him. He noticed she didn't take advantage of several opportunities to put her elbows and knees in places that might have caused him serious pain. Maybe that was a good sign. Or maybe she was just a nice person.

By the time she'd reclaimed Joey and calmed him down, said thank you to the elderly man who'd caught the kid, and found a way to straighten her own disheveled clothes, Morgan had reorganized the stroller so she could strap a still cranky Joey into place and hand him a hard, fat cookie.

Morgan expected her to walk off the moment Joey was settled, but instead she sat, or collapsed, back down on the bench. She pulled a bottle of water out of a hidden pocket in the diaper bag and took a long drink.

"I'm afraid I only have one of these," she apologized.

"I need something a little stronger right now, anyway."

She gave him a sharp look and took another drink before she capped off the bottle and hid it away again. "So, why *are* you in L.A. this time?"

Okay, she'd given him another chance. He hoped he'd be able to convert it into a win, for his own sake as much as Joey's.

Morgan was too close. Rosalie could feel the heat of his body, smell the blend of musk and sex that was uniquely his, and see the tension in the muscular shoulders hidden under his black polo shirt. She shifted away under the pretense of taking a board-book out of Joey's bag and handed it to him.

"I'm in town to give you an update on the custody situation." Morgan's business-like tone rasped against her already-raw nerves.

"Which you can't do by phone?" She stood up so abruptly she dropped the diaper bag on the ground. "This isn't a good time. I need to get Joey home, and . . ."

Morgan bent to pick up the bag and stowed it under the stroller.

"Can I buy you lunch?"

"What is this compulsion you have to feed me? It's not as if I'm too thin."

"You're the perfect shape for a woman, but I think the kid may be hungry."

Joey had the corner of the book in his mouth and was chewing on it thoughtfully.

"He's got a tooth coming in." She dug around in the back of the stroller for another teething cracker, ignoring the heat on her face and the tendrils of pleasure his compliment planted in her heart.

"But you have to eat. And I have to eat. Why not eat together?"

She handed Joey the cracker, her mind whirling too fast to find an answer.

Even if Morgan didn't take her by surprise when he'd showed up with his stepmother, she hadn't been prepared for the full impact of the encounter. She'd suspected her body would betray her, would heat and tingle under his gaze, his touch. But she hadn't expected her heart to ache with a longing to be in his arms that had nothing to do with sex and everything to do with the man she'd thought he was. The man whose image had disrupted her dreams for the last week. The man she'd missed so much.

Tears of frustration with herself, as much as anything, burned behind her eyes.

Damn. Morgan could see the tears Rosalie refused to let fall.

He'd expected her to be angry with him, after how he'd blown it the last time he saw her, but not sad, not like this. It'd never occurred to him he might be able to make her cry. He'd never let anyone, any woman, get that close before.

The women he dated were well aware of where he stood. Since what they wanted from him was some combination of his prestige, his wealth, and reliably good sex, they had no problem with it. They all knew he didn't do relationships.

Until he'd met Rosalie. This woman, and the kid, made the prospect of . . . many years with her far more attractive than he'd ever have expected.

But the tears, and the power over her he hadn't known he had, changed all that. Now he needed to walk away before he hurt her anymore.

He was half-way to his feet, "Goodbye" half-way to his lips when Joey reached out a damp, messy hand and grabbed a pudgy handful of his best pair of five-hundred-dollar jeans.

"Mawg?"

Morgan sank back. He'd forgotten what was at stake here.

Rosalie was a strong woman. He hated knowing he'd probably hurt her someday, but she'd be able to deal with it. Joey was a little kid. He needed Morgan to look out for him. Walking away wasn't an option.

Across the plaza, the mariachi band finished a Mexican ballad to scattered applause.

"This isn't a good place for an update on the custody battle," he pointed out.

No place with Joey around would be. Besides, he needed to regroup, rethink how to win her over.

"And I'd rather not explain it on the phone," he went on. "If you can't do lunch, maybe we could have dinner tonight?"

"Feeding me again?" She gave him a lopsided smile.

"It's traditional. You know, caveman brings mammoth steak back to cave."

"Mammoth steak? Oh, yum."

Her smile faded. He watched the mental battle he could see so clearly in her eyes, not sure which side he wanted to win until she said, "Yes."

His heart gave a little jump of triumph. "Seven o'clock?"

*

Why, why, why did she agree to have dinner with Morgan? Rosalie did not need to go through all that again. What kind of idiot was she?

The kind who'd spent most of her life hoping against hope things would turn out the way she wanted them to, just once. And here she was again, caught in the same old trap.

At least he'd changed the invitation from lunch to dinner. They'd eat and talk, period. Jill was free to sit with Joey, which provided Rosalie with the perfect excuse to make a quick escape.

Morgan didn't say where they were going, and she didn't have the nerve to call and ask, so while Joey napped she stared for a long time at the line of dark suits in her closet, but the perfect dress didn't miraculously appear.

She ignored the flowered dresses gathered at one end of the rack. Vanessa was right. Flowers were not her. Some other time she'd figure out why it had taken her so long to realize that.

The only flower-free dresses she owned were the blue chambray, the black halter, and a dark green silk shirtwaist she wore to weddings. Why not wear the shirtwaist to dinner with Morgan? The irony might serve as a counter-weight to her over-eager heart in case he repeated his crazy proposal.

She refused to think about what Vanessa had said about men and buttons. Or how true it had turned out to be.

Morgan was right on time again, but of course Jill wasn't.

"I'm running late," Rosalie explained when she opened the door in her bathrobe and high heels. "I should have remembered the Jill factor—always allow an extra fifteen minutes."

"No problem. I can watch Joey until she gets here or you finish getting . . ."

She felt her face go red at her half-naked state.

" . . . ready," he finished.

"I'm afraid I was using the electronic babysitter while I got ready." Her hand went to the carefully structured hairdo she'd somehow managed to create.

"Electronic babysitter? I didn't know technology had gone quite that far."

"You'd call it a television."

"Oh." He grinned at her and her foolish heart bounced in her chest.

To distract herself she took note of the dark suit he wore. The ironic green-silk dress would be fine.

"You can watch with him. Are you a Sesame Street fan?"

"Can't say I am. But I could learn." Again that grin.

Just then Jill sprinted up the walk and screeched to a halt in the doorway.

"Sorry I'm late. Wow, quite a fashion statement there, Rosalie. Hi, Mr. Hottie."

A flush crept across Morgan's face. "Er, hi, Jill."

Rosalie managed not to laugh. "I guess I forgot to introduce you the last time. Jill, this is Mr. Danby."

"Whatever," the girl replied. "Where's my main squeeze?"

"Watching TV. Why don't you tell Mr. Danby about your soccer team's trip to Sacramento?"

"Huh? Sure. Okay. I just gotta get a snack."

Jill led Morgan toward the kitchen as she chattered full speed. Rosalie checked to make sure Joey was content in his playpen, fascinated by the numbers that danced across the television screen, before she rushed to her room.

She emerged ten minutes later to find Joey on Jill's hip, while Morgan snapped a picture of them on Jill's cell phone, and Smudge and Sylvester wound around the legs of his black suit.

"Oooh, cool. Thanks, Mr. D." The girl plopped Joey back into the playpen and grabbed the cell. "Gotta send it to my friends. He's sooo cute."

"It runs in the family." Morgan gave Rosalie a look of well-banked desire. "Or not in the family exactly, but you know what I mean."

"Thank you. Will I need a wrap of some kind?"

She hoped not, since she didn't have one that went with the dress, but she also didn't want to have to borrow his jacket again if they went to the beach.

He shook his head. "It's quite pleasant out."

It was, she discovered when she'd told Jill they'd be back before her midnight curfew, kissed Joey, and let Morgan gesture her out the door ahead of him.

The flower-scented night wasn't too warm. The breeze off the ocean was gentle. The sky was a soft violet, edging into hyacinth overhead, and full of stars.

Then she noticed the car parked at the curb.

"A Rolls?"

He chuckled as he opened the car door for her. "Why not?"

By the time he got in beside her, she'd figured it out.

"You rented the Rolls to drive Lillian around, didn't you?"

"No. I chose it to drive you around. You forget I didn't expect Lillian to be here."

She closed her eyes and sank into his words for a moment. The smell of the leather seats mixed with his sexy scent. The purr of the engine blended with the softness of the night air. Her body felt languid, half-asleep, and yet strangely alive, with tingles and tugs in secret places.

He turned out onto the boulevard and Rosalie surrendered to reality. "Why is she here?"

"I haven't a clue. She said she wanted to see Joey before she made a final decision about suing for custody. I hoped he'd be difficult but, of course, he was sweet and adorable."

"She didn't even want to hold him."

"He does tend to be sticky."

Rosalie cast him a sidelong look of disgust.

"Hey, don't ask me to explain Lillian to you. I don't pretend to understand her myself."

"It's almost as if he's a possession she feels she has to own, not a child. That's sad, and a little scary."

"Uh-huh."

His tone reminded her Lillian was the woman who had raised him. And Charlie. Maybe she'd been more maternal when she was younger. Or maybe not.

"Where are we having dinner?" she asked to change the subject.

"My condo."

She jerked around in her seat to face him. "You're taking me to your place again?"

"It's quiet, and I have a wonderful caterer."

He also had a very large, very comfortable bed, Rosalie remembered with a shiver of desire she couldn't deny.

"Don't worry. I wouldn't ever make you do anything you didn't want to do."

The problem wasn't what she wanted to do but what she didn't dare allow herself to do.

"I will *not* have sex with you again tonight." She half expected him to point out she hadn't been invited to, but instead he shook his head.

"Was the last time so awful?"

She turned away. "No, but . . ."

"Believe me, sex with you is the furthest thing from my mind right now."

She raised one eyebrow and he shrugged.

"Okay, maybe not the furthest, but not at the top of the list, either."

She didn't want to think about where on the list it might be. She closed her eyes and let the luxury of the car and Mozart on the sound system carry her away.

When they reached the condo she strolled past the leather-

and-chrome sofa to gaze in wonder out the floor-to-ceiling window at the colorful lights of her city.

"Would you like a glass of wine before dinner?" Morgan asked. "Since I ordered prime rib, I opened a bottle of red to let it breathe before I went to pick you up."

She swallowed and stepped away from the window. "Sure."

She didn't watch as he poured the wine, but chose a modernistic leather armchair and set her purse on the table next to it. The leather felt cool on her legs, but its soft, sensuous texture seemed to caress her through the silk.

So this was what it was like, not to splurge once in a while, but to be rich all the time. She wasn't sure she liked it. She certainly didn't feel comfortable surrounded by all this luxury.

She didn't, in fact, feel comfortable at all. Part of it was the awareness that she was alone with Morgan and his bed was a few feet, or given the size of the penthouse, a few yards away. And part of the discomfort was the hot tug of need deep inside her and the prickle of excitement along her skin. Nerves, she told herself.

Rosalie was nervous. For some reason he couldn't have explained, Morgan found that charming. He handed her a glass of the Château Lafite Rothschild and was charmed all over again by the surprise on her face when she took her first sip.

"What is it? It's like liquid music. I've never tasted anything like it before."

He chuckled.

"Is it a ridiculously expensive French wine?" She wrinkled her nose and looked more intently at the ruby-red liquid.

"Just enjoy." He sat on the end of the sofa nearest her chair and tried to decide on the right topic for small-talk.

"So, what was this update about the custody case you came here to give me?" Rosalie asked before he came up with one.

Okay, no small-talk.

"Charlie's father is out of the picture."

"I thought he was all along."

"There was always a chance, a small one, but I made sure he understood once and for all it would cost him far more to pursue custody than he wanted to pay."

He waited, for thanks maybe, but she took another sip of her wine and continued to stare out the window at the blinking city lights.

"Why did you ask me to marry you?"

The question seemed to startle her as much as it startled him.

"Because I want to be married to you."

"You can't. I mean, you might want to have sex with me, but you can't want to marry a woman you hardly know."

"I know you well enough to think it'll work out okay. We can learn more about each other after we're married."

She gave a huff of laughter. "I still don't buy it, Morgan. Why marriage?"

He stared into his glass, rolling the wine around in it while he rolled ways to avoid the question around in his head. In the end he decided to tell her the truth.

"It worked for my father and Lillian. She didn't have much money of her own and had been so eager to get free from Paul Thompson she'd settled for less than she should have in their divorce. Plus, she needed a place to live where he couldn't get at her. My father was a few years older, but they'd traveled in the same social circles all their lives. Since my mother left us, er, him, about the same time Lillian left Thompson, it made sense for them to get married to quiet the gossip on both fronts."

Rosalie's face showed clearly what she thought of such a dreary reason to get married. Still, all he could do was push ahead.

"I want to keep you in my life, and I don't want you and Lillian to end up in court over Joey. If we get married and adopt him, Lillian will back off. Hence, marriage looks to be the logical solution in our case too."

Rosalie went rigid and set her wine glass down. "Nice Spock imitation."

Morgan laughed in spite of himself.

"It's logical if you only consider what you want," she agreed, "but did you ever consider what anyone else might want? Me, for instance."

"You want to keep Joey."

"And I want to keep my life." She knotted her hands in her lap. "I spent a lot of years trying not to get lost in someone else's needs. My mom wanted that for me too, but it was a perpetual battle for both of us. It took so much of my time to help her live her life."

Finally she looked up at him, her eyes glistening.

"Now I've built my own life, why would I just want to be Joey's mom and your lover? What happens after you lose interest in me?"

He cleared his throat. "I don't plan to lose interest."

Another small laugh, like breaking glass this time.

"My father didn't plan on my mother's illness, either. When she got too sick, he did what men do. He walked."

"Women walk too," Morgan countered before he could stop himself.

Rosalie started to protest, then remembered how many times she'd already tried to walk away from this man. And failed.

"I won't marry you," she told him. "If you can't talk Lillian out of the custody suit, I'll fight her and I'll win. I don't need you to keep him, any more than you need me to . . ."

He raised one eyebrow. "To have a satisfying sex life?"

"Something like that."

A discreet noise from the doorway announced their dinner was ready. Morgan thanked the uniformed older woman and held out his hand to help Rosalie to her feet.

She shook her head and stood on her own. She'd be fine as

long as he didn't touch her, as long as her body had no chance to give in to the simmering heat between them.

The dining room didn't have as spectacular a view, but it did have a small Monet centered on the wall at one end. An original, she'd guess, based on a lifetime of trips to the local museums and galleries with her mother.

Morgan held a chair out for her, then sat across the table from her.

"I hope you enjoy the meal."

She more than enjoyed the food. She felt as if she'd fallen into some kind of culinary heaven. The thin slices of perfectly cooked beef were laid across a creamy polenta and drizzled with red, white, and green sauces, each more sublime than the last. She managed to stifle most of her moans of delight, but couldn't stop herself from closing her eyes occasionally in pure bliss.

The conversation did proper homage to the delicious meal. They talked about whatever came to mind—the Monet, local museums they were both familiar with, other cities they'd visited, or rather, he'd visited and she'd dreamed of visiting.

When he got up to take another bottle off the rack on the sideboard, she realized she'd let herself be seduced by the silky luxury of the wine and had more than her usual single glass.

"No more for me, thank you."

He nodded and sat down as the caterer came to clear their plates.

Rosalie leaned back in her chair. "So, you came all the way to Los Angeles to tell me you'd taken Charlie's father out of the hunt?"

He drained the last of his wine. "I also came to tell you that I want to keep you in my life. If not as my wife, at least as my 'main squeeze', I think Jill called it."

"You mean your girlfriend?" *Your mistress?*

"My lover."

The words were a dash of cold water that sobered her instantly.

153

Sobered her, and yet sent sweet tendrils of desire creeping through all the secret parts of her body.

Maybe an affair was the solution. If she knew from the start she couldn't trust him to stay, maybe she could find a way to survive when he walked away. Or maybe not. She needed time and space to consider the possibility without Morgan's distracting presence, without the sweet flames inside her body that made it hard to think at all.

The server reappeared from the kitchen with their dessert. "Coffee?"

"Yes, please." Morgan looked across at Rosalie. "You?"

She never drank coffee at dinner, but this seemed like an excellent time to break the rule. She needed to be awake and alert to deal with Morgan. "Yes, please. Black."

The dessert was more divine than the prime rib. What appeared to be a chocolate cupcake with fudge frosting turned out to be a mocha confection filled with raspberry-flavored whipped cream. They showed it proper respect by eating in a comfortable silence.

"Excellent meal," Morgan told the server when she came to clear the table.

"Yes, delicious." Rosalie sighed. "I should go home."

"It's early yet." His voice was a purr as dark and rich as the coffee, as intoxicating as the wine. "We haven't had much opportunity to talk to each other. Who knows, given the chance, you might even begin to like me."

"I like you." Too damn much. "But I still think maybe it's better if you take me home."

He came around and pulled her chair out. She stood and found him so close all she could see was his silk shirt and a vintage tie hand-painted by a famous rock star.

Her breath stopped, then came out in a gasp of . . . Surprise, she told herself.

She tried to back away, forgetting the table, and lost her

balance. His hands, with those long, strong fingers, caught her by the shoulders.

A wave of sexual awareness washed over her and threatened to pull her into an undertow of sensations and emotions that might drown her. Rosalie looked up into Morgan's eyes.

"Steady," he said in the same seductive purr.

"I . . ." She shivered.

He took her in his arms and held her gently against the solid strength of his body clothed in the softness of fine wool and silk. She couldn't remember when she'd felt so safe, so sheltered. With a sigh, she laid her head on his chest.

"Rosalie," he laid his cheek on the top of her head, "please stay. Just for a while."

She never wanted to move, much less leave. Unable, maybe unwilling, to put her emotions into words, she nodded.

He released her slowly, then took her by the hand.

His touch had as powerful an effect on her as she'd feared. It was like the magical moment when she found the exact piece of legal information she needed to be sure she'd win her case, multiplied by a thousand. Multiplied by a thousand, and spread through her whole body, a white light that lit her from within and made every bit of her tingly and more alive than she'd ever been before.

She should have left while she had the chance, but she couldn't be sorry she'd stayed.

Morgan led Rosalie to the living room, not sure which of them was more nervous. He sat at one end of the sofa and tucked her under his arm. She settled there with another of those breathy little sighs, her head on his shoulder, her hand still in his.

He lifted her hand to his lips and kissed it, then rested it on his thigh. Unsure of what to say, he asked, "Why do you paint your toes, but not your fingernails?"

She snatched her hand away. "I don't wear sandals to work."

"Ah. Ever the professional. Good thing. Who knows what effect those sexy little toes of yours might have in court."

"My toes are not sexy."

He took her hand from her lap and kissed it again. "Let me be the judge of what's sexy."

He traced a line across her hand with his finger. Her breath hitched. He kissed the center of her palm. She gave a tiny gasp. He lifted one finger and nibbled at the tip. Her hand tensed, as if to pull away, but after a moment relaxed back into his.

Reminding himself to go slow, he kissed her hand again before he set it back in her lap. The gesture accomplished what he'd meant it to—she turned toward him.

Very slowly he lifted his hand to her chin and tilted her face up to his. Her eyes widened. He had to suppress a groan when her tongue slid out to lick her lips in silent invitation. Gently he lowered his mouth to hers.

Oh, yes! The shock of heat and hunger rocketed through him. Better, he felt it rocket through Rosalie's body, too.

She went tense in his arms, but only to draw closer to him. Her hand went to his shoulder, teased the sensitive skin at the back of his neck. Her hips pressed hard against his leg in one wanton pulse before she could stop herself, and he smiled against her lips as a wave of tenderness swept over him that made it easier to rein in the demands of his own body and focus on her needs.

The heat of Morgan's kiss flowed through Rosalie like warm honey, relaxing every muscle. She feared she might melt away entirely until he plunged his tongue into her mouth.

Languid enchantment was replaced with an explosion of pleasure and hunger. Her hands tightened on his neck, her chest pressed closer against his. She could feel the unfamiliar power of her femininity in the tremor of his hands, the roughness of his breath, the hardness of his body.

156

They floated sideways on a golden cloud of discovery and delight until they lay on the couch with him on top of her. She held her breath for a moment before she sank into the rightness of it. The rightness of him.

Chapter Eleven

Morgan's kisses became more urgent. The tugs and tension inside Rosalie's core became more urgent too. One of his hands slid down her body to press her center more firmly into him.

She was glad his weight kept her from surrendering to the need to writhe under him in an attempt to reach for something shiny and special that hovered in the bright heat between them.

When his hand moved up to take hold of her breast she gasped out loud and felt the tiny huff of his laughter on her lips. She arched her head back in timeless invitation as his hand kneaded the sensitive flesh it held.

His groan rumbled against her chest. The sound sent an erotic tremor through her, magnified by caresses that touched all the right places, to open new doors of unexpected delight.

He caught her pebbled nipple between his fingers and the pleasure became so intense she almost had to pull away.

He must have sensed the hovering edge of pain because, with obvious reluctance, his lips left hers, traced a line of sparks down her cheek to her ear. She cried out softly when he nipped at the tender lobe. He sighed and lifted himself to his elbows over her.

"Shall we move this someplace a little more comfortable?"

"Um?" She forced her groggy mind to focus.

"We'd be more comfortable in the bedroom."

"Yes."

He shifted to sit beside her. Cool air and cold reality flowed into the space between them.

"No!" She took a deep breath. "I mean, yes, we'd be more comfortable there, but I don't think . . ."

He smiled and moved closer again. "Don't think."

"Joey." She struggled to clear her mind from the intoxicating effects of his nearness. "Jill."

She took a gulp of air and pressed one hand against his chest. He sat up at once and smiled down at her.

"You're right." He took her hand and kissed it again, then glanced at the clock over the fireplace. "We need to get you home before your babysitter turns into a pumpkin."

He helped her sit up and watched with a grin while she tried to put her clothes into some sort of order.

When she was sure her wobbly knees would hold her, she stood and gathered up her purse, to hold it like a shield in front of her.

They rode down to the garage in silence. She should have felt awkward—more than awkward—but she didn't. She felt exhilarated, alive.

They talked about little nothings on the drive back to her house. Morgan didn't seem to mind that she'd called a halt to their evening. He was as charming as ever, but the charm had a new air of intimacy that made it even more irresistible.

She hardly noticed where they were until the car pulled up in front of her house. She turned to say goodbye and found he'd leaned closer to her. Much closer.

She looked at the house to make sure Jill wasn't watching, blinked, then looked again.

All the lights were off. A quick glance at the car's clock showed it wasn't Jill's curfew yet. Had the babysitter gone to sleep on the

159

sofa? Unlikely, when she had the chance to watch unlimited television. Where was she? More important, where was Joey?

"Joey!"

Rosalie opened the car door and raced mindlessly up the path.

Morgan caught up with her as she fumbled with the door keys and took them from her to unlock the door.

The moment she stepped inside she knew the house was empty, except for the cats asleep on the sofa, but she searched every room to be sure, Morgan silent in her wake.

Back in the front hall, heart pounding, stomach in full rebellion, she took out her cell and pushed Jill's button.

"'Lo," a sleepy voice greeted her.

"Jill! Where are you?"

"Home. Asleep. Rosalie? What's up?"

Cold, dark suspicion crept up Rosalie's spine. Instinctively she turned her back to Morgan and bent over the cell, as if to keep him from hearing what came next. Oh, lord, what came next?

"Where's Joey?"

"With his grandma. She came to pick him up, with the nanny, like you told her to, when you decided to spend the night . . ." The girl stopped. "But you wouldn't do that, would you?" Rosalie felt her face go red at the memory of how close she'd come, but fear and anger swept every thought away, except one. Lillian had Joey.

"Did I screw up?" Jill asked in a small voice.

"It wasn't your fault. Go back to sleep."

Rosalie clicked off. She knew whose fault it was.

Anger swelled inside her as she turned toward Morgan.

"You son of a bitch!"

He jerked back in surprise.

"Don't act innocent, you unspeakable jerk."

"What happened?"

"As if you didn't know. Lillian has Joey. Where the hell did she take him?"

*

Rage cascaded down Morgan's body, washing away the worry over the kid that had all but paralyzed him. "You think I knew about this?"

"No, I don't think you knew about this. I think you planned it. Why else would you put on the big seduction act? You gave yourself too much credit, as usual, and thought I wouldn't find out that she'd taken him until tomorrow. Now, where's Joey?"

"I don't know."

She took a step toward him and jabbed her finger inches from his chest. The urge to swipe her hand away trembled through him, but he ignored it.

"Don't lie to me. Where did she take him?"

"Back to Boston, probably." The implications of what Lillian had done hit him like a bucket of ice-cold water. "We've got to stop her."

Rosalie's cell phone was already in her hand.

"The police will find them."

"You'd call the police on Lillian?"

"The woman kidnapped my son. Kidnapping's a crime. Someone commits a crime, you call the police. You don't have to go to law school to know that."

He reached out and closed his hand over hers, surprised to find it ice cold. "You can't."

She jerked her hand away. "Why not? I want Joey back. Now."

"I'll get him back for you. Leave the police out of it. If I don't have him back by morning, you can call them then."

She rolled her eyes. "And look like a besotted fool who waited until it was too late to report a crime because some man told her he'd take care of it? No, thank you. She, and you, did the crime. You can both do the time."

"How will that be better for Joey? Will it get him home any faster?"

She grimaced and turned off the phone. Relief made him take a step back.

161

"Please stop pretending you weren't in on this." The hint of tears in her voice softened the blow of her accusation. But not enough.

"You really believe I'd help Lillian do something this stupid?"

"You ask me out to dinner and play the seduction game, she walks off with Joey. Jill said she even brought a nanny with her. Sounds as if it was all planned out in advance."

He took another deep breath. "Not by me. All I know is Lillian wanted to have dinner with me. I told her I had a dinner date with you. There was no mention, no sign, of a nanny."

"How did Lillian find my address?"

"Maybe her lawyer dug it up. I don't know."

"You keep saying you don't know, but you're also pretty darn sure you can find them and bring Joey back."

She wasn't being rational. He'd never known what to do when logical arguments didn't work. Arguments about why his mother shouldn't leave, arguments about why Rosalie should believe him. Believe in him. The rage pushed him toward the door, but raw emotion wasn't the answer. He'd learned that much.

"Why don't you let me at least try?"

"Where do you think they are?" she asked in a small voice.

"They might be on their way back to Boston, but Lillian's not the type to take the red-eye. Maybe we should sit down and . . ." Rosalie took three awkward steps and fell more than sat in one of the dining-room chairs. The cats came to stand silent guard at her feet.

He sat across from her, took out his cell, and punched in the familiar number. The phone at the other end rang three times before Lillian's butler answered.

"Harkins? I need to know what day Mrs. Danby's scheduled to leave Los Angeles."

He shot a glance at Rosalie, who looked as if she'd fall apart at any moment. Lillian wouldn't harm Joey, but Rosalie wouldn't find that much comfort. She wanted her kid back. He didn't blame her.

"I know it's late there, Harkins, but this is urgent."

As the anger ebbed, fear took over. Rosalie wrapped her arms around her waist and sat shaking while Morgan listened to the voice on the phone.

Too many strong emotions swirled around inside her. Too many awful images flowed through her brain. She fought to focus on Morgan's words, on anything real and stable.

"Well, wake the whole staff, if you have to." She shuddered at Morgan's subdued roar, glad she wasn't the person on the other end. "Someone must know her itinerary."

He crossed one long leg over the other and jiggled his foot while he waited to have his orders obeyed.

If only she could think straight. But Joey's absence was like a hole in the center of her body that sucked in all her energy and left room for nothing else.

Coffee. She should make coffee. She started to stand, but her legs wouldn't hold her.

When she wobbled, Morgan took her hand in his free one to steady her. His touch didn't sizzle, the way it had earlier, but sent a slow warmth though her as she lowered herself back into the chair.

She wasn't alone. Tears flooded down her face. She pulled her hand free to wipe them away, then wished she hadn't. She didn't want him to see how shattered she was.

She didn't feel so cold, so afraid when he held her hand, but that made no sense. He was obviously angry with her.

But he was still here to help her. Or to help Lillian.

She wished she could put two thoughts together without thinking about Joey, worrying whether he was okay.

Morgan straightened. "Thank you, Harkins. If it hadn't been an emergency, I wouldn't have bothered you."

"What did you find out?" Rosalie's heart hammered in her chest.

"They're not due to leave until tomorrow." He stood up and took out the car keys. "I'll drive out to her hotel and have Joey back in an hour or two."

"No."

Now it was clear what needed to be done, everything was easier. She stood on solid legs, grabbed her purse, and headed for her bedroom.

"I'll go with you. Just let me get a coat. I don't want Joey alone with strangers any longer than he has to be."

"Are you sure . . .?"

"Yes. The woman has my son."

The drive to Santa Monica seemed endless. When they got to the hotel Morgan tossed the car keys to the valet and led her inside.

Despite the late hour, the brightly lit lobby was full of people talking, laughing. Didn't they know someone had taken her child? She shook the reaction off. She'd felt the same way during the dark last days of her mother's illness.

Morgan must have known Lillian's room number because he headed through the crowd to the bank of elevators.

The close confines of the metal box made it impossible to ignore his tension—or his anger. Rosalie shivered.

She heard the muted sound of Joey's wail the minute they stepped off the elevator. Her body tensed. Charlie's face, his father's face, flashed through her mind.

No, she reminded herself. But the mere idea made her grab Morgan's arm. She didn't realize how tightly until he twisted it to loosen her grip.

"Sorry," she mumbled past the lump in her throat.

To her surprise, the door to Lillian's suite opened as soon as Morgan knocked.

"You're not room service," Lillian snapped at him.

"No, but you *are* in the middle of committing a felony."

Rosalie pushed past Morgan into the suite.

"Why is she here?" Lillian asked.

"Where's the kid?" Morgan countered, but Rosalie didn't wait for an answer.

She followed Joey's wail across the room toward a closed door and threw it open.

On the other side, a sturdy young woman in a gray uniform stood by a crib with Joey in her arms. He wriggled and kicked so hard, Rosalie didn't see how the woman could hold on.

When she saw Rosalie, the nanny cooed, "Who's that?" over his protests.

Rosalie crossed the room and took the boy into her arms. The familiar weight, his little-boy smell were like magical gifts after all she'd been through in the last hour.

"Oh, sweetie." She hugged him close. "Are you okay?"

He stopped crying and laid his head on her shoulder. "Mama."

She froze, unable to breathe, her heart too big for her chest. He'd never called her "Mama" before.

"Yes, Joey, I'm here."

"Mrs. Danby tried to get him to call her Mama, but he wouldn't." The nanny's relief was obvious. "That's when I figured out there might be a custody issue here. I didn't know whether or not to call 911."

Rosalie kissed the top of Joey's head, almost drowning in relief. Now he was quiet, she heard the low, angry rumble of Morgan's voice in the next room. He didn't yell, but his tone still made her glad she couldn't hear his exact words. She exchanged nervous glances with the nanny.

"Can you help me gather up Joey's things?" Rosalie asked her.

The nanny nodded and began to gather the toys he'd thrown around the room.

"Joey?" she said. "Mrs. Danby called him Charlie."

Rosalie groaned and held the child closer.

By the time the nanny had everything organized, Joey was asleep. Rosalie managed to get him strapped in the shiny new car seat without waking him. All she heard now from the next room were Lillian's sobs. Rosalie and the nanny exchanged another nervous look.

"Maybe I should call someone to carry him downstairs for you," the nanny suggested.

"I'll carry him." Morgan stood in the doorway.

He seemed older, the lines in his face clearer, his eyes dim.

"I've arranged another room in the hotel for you," he told the nanny, "and pre-paid a shuttle to the airport in the morning. Here's my business card with your airline reservation number on it, and my cell, so you can call me if you have problems with Mrs. Danby. Call me, too, if you don't receive the money she owes you within a week. You can use me for a reference. I'm sorry you got dragged into this."

"I'm sorry, too. I had no idea . . ." The nanny turned to Rosalie. "Your son's such a sweet little thing, and so cute. You're a lucky lady."

Rosalie laid a hand on Joey's head to reassure herself again he was safe.

The nanny picked up her suitcase and coat, cast one worried glance toward the next room, and left by a door that opened into the hotel hallway.

Before Rosalie was able to decide what to do or say next, fists pounded on the main door to the suite.

"Open up! Police!"

Lillian screamed. Something heavy fell to the floor.

"Stay here!" Morgan ordered Rosalie.

He rushed into the next room at the same moment three police officers burst in through the door to the hall, guns drawn. Instinctively he froze and raised his hands, then took an involuntary step forward at the sight of Lillian sprawled unconscious on the floor.

One of the officers, a woman, clicked the radio on her shoulder to call for an ambulance.

"Who are you?" one of the male officers asked, gun still pointed at Morgan's heart.

Morgan explained, his mind half on the gun, half on Lillian as the other two officers assessed her condition.

Satisfied there were no weapons in the room, the officer interrogating Morgan lowered his weapon while the other male officer gave Lillian CPR.

Morgan stood where he could watch their progress while he answered questions. Slowly Lillian's face, so twisted with pain he barely recognized it, went from gray to something more like its usual color.

"And where's the child now?" the officer asked.

Morgan gestured toward the bedroom. "In there with his legal guardian."

The officer flipped back a few pages in his notebook. "Ms. Walker?"

Awareness dawned. Rage robbed Morgan of the breath to answer. Rosalie not only thought he'd been in on Lillian's plot, she'd called the police after all.

He nodded and relaxed the hands that had fisted at his side.

At a signal from the officer in charge, the female officer knocked once on the door and went into the other room.

Rosalie answered the officer's questions, then waited in awkward silence with her until they heard the EMTs roll the gurney with Lillian on it to the elevator.

One of the male officers came in. "Ready to go?" he asked his colleague.

The female officer turned to Rosalie. "Do you have a way to get home?"

The image of dollar signs flying away danced in Rosalie's mind as she imagined what a cab would cost. She was about to ask the officer if taxis took credit cards when Morgan reappeared at the bedroom door.

"I'll take them home."

"Didn't you ride in the ambulance with Lillian?" Rosalie asked in surprise.

"I'll swing by the hospital later."

"If you're sure . . ." the female officer said to Rosalie.

In spite of the tight mask of rage on his face, the certainty that Morgan would never harm her remained.

She nodded and the two officers went back into the other room, where the one who seemed to be in charge was deep in conversation with the hotel manager.

Morgan bent to pick Joey's car seat up. "If I get this, can you get everything else?" he asked Rosalie, without looking at her.

"Shouldn't you be with your stepmother?"

"My stepmother can go to hell, for all I care." He opened the door and waited while Rosalie picked up Joey's bag, then headed down the hall.

She'd been wrong, terribly wrong, about him. But his icy tone and rigid posture didn't invite an apology, and she was too drained to attempt one she doubted he'd even listen to.

"Will Lillian be okay?" Rosalie rushed to keep up with his long, angry strides.

"She's stabilized. The medics told me it was a minor heart attack. She should be okay." He punched the button for the elevator. "Why do you care, anyway?"

Because she's all the family you have, Rosalie wanted to say, but she used the arrival of the elevator as an excuse not to say anything at all.

She had Joey back, for good now. Wasn't that what mattered?

*

Morgan stared out the condo window. He took a sip of whiskey and noted the time. Three a.m. The hospital had sent him home a little after two with promises Lillian was well on her way to a full recovery. Someday he might be glad, but right now he couldn't find it in him to care.

Below him Los Angeles was at low ebb. This wasn't a twenty-four-hour-a-day city like New York, but the traffic never stopped completely either. Like Boston. Not "like home." He'd lived all his life in Boston, but home meant a place where you belonged. He didn't belong anywhere, or with anyone.

After tonight he wouldn't be welcome anymore in the house where his family had lived for four generations. He'd inherit it after Lillian died, but he'd shared the house with Charlie for too many years to imagine living there again.

And Rosalie didn't want to raise Joey in his condo.

The expression on her face as she'd tucked the kid back in his own crib a few hours earlier floated through Morgan's mind. He didn't belong with her, with them, either, he reminded himself. She'd made that very clear. His hand tightened on the glass.

She'd actually believed he would help Lillian take Joey away from her. She'd believed he'd planned the whole thing. She'd believed he would have made love to her to move the plot along. He hadn't bothered to point out to her how crazy all that was. Either she trusted him, or she didn't.

Obviously, she didn't.

And he couldn't trust her now, either.

Not after she'd broken her word and called the police on a sad old woman whose only mistake was a chronic inability to take no for an answer.

He'd seen them home, seen Joey safe in his crib, and left. She'd tried to thank him, but he'd ignored her. He'd done what he'd done for Joey's sake, not hers.

This time he'd been the one who walked away.

His cell phone buzzed in his pocket. He didn't need to look

to know it was Rosalie. She'd been calling ever since he'd walked out her door, but he had nothing to say to her.

Still, after the cell went quiet he felt even more alone.

Rosalie woke up the next morning groggy from lack of sleep, but more than happy to have Joey home, never mind that he was groggy too, and grumpy with it.

She got him washed and dressed, fixed his breakfast, and made herself coffee before she called Morgan's cell phone one more time, in case he'd turned it off the night before.

No answer. His refusal to listen crawled deep down into her heart to chill her very core despite the sunshine of Joey's chatter as he ate.

She should just let it go. Morgan had clearly been furious she thought he'd helped Lillian take Joey, and in a rage that she'd called the police after he'd asked her not to. He'd refused to listen to let her explain she'd been afraid Lillian might have taken Joey to another hotel. If she had, they'd never have found them before their flight left, without police help.

He'd ignored her pleas and left, the way she'd always known he would. It was over.

Joey threw his bowl on the floor to announce he'd finished his breakfast and was still feeling the adverse effects of a late night.

She picked the bowl up, wiped up the mess, and cleaned the tray on his highchair, then dampened a wash cloth to wipe his face. Normally she'd put him in his playpen next and eat her own breakfast, but today she wanted to throw the cereal bowl on the floor herself.

She kept seeing the look on Morgan's face when he'd walked out the door. He'd been in such a dark place and totally alone, even his tie to Lillian severed, at least for now.

For some reason she didn't understand, she needed to know he was all right.

Against her better judgment she picked up her cell. This time she texted with fingers that shook so much she could barely type, "R U OK?"

She didn't want to disrupt Joey's routine, so she resisted the urge to keep him safe near her every minute and put him in his playpen. She forced herself to go back to the kitchen and eat a slice of toast to cushion the black coffee.

Ten minutes later her cell announced a text. Hands trembling, she opened it.

"I'm fine. Why shouldn't I be?" Morgan had written.

She turned off her cell with a "click!" that seemed to echo around the kitchen.

Okay, now it was over for good.

What a hell of a time to realize she was in love with Morgan Danby.

Morgan paced the hospital corridor just before noon, trying not to remember the night his father died. Luckily, he didn't have to wait long before a nurse appeared to show him to Lillian's room.

Reclined in the big white bed without her makeup, designer suits, and diamonds, his stepmother looked like a sick old woman.

Her eyes fluttered open. "I didn't expect you to come."

He almost hadn't, but she had no one else to watch out for her. He sat on the chair beside the bed and forced himself to take her bony hand in his.

"Are you feeling okay?"

She nodded, as if talking were too much of an effort.

"Are you in any pain?"

She shook her head.

"Do you need anything? Want anything?"

"I want to go home." A tear ran down her cheek.

"We'll get you home as soon as we can." He shifted uneasily in his chair. "Did the doctor say how long it will be before you're released from the hospital?"

She frowned. "I don't remember."

"That's probably because of the drugs, er, medicine they gave you."

Her hand clutched at his. "Are you very angry with me?"

"Yes."

"Mr. Danby," a nurse said from the doorway. "The doctor is here and can talk to you now about your mother's condition."

"My stepmother," he corrected. He stood and set Lillian's hand back on the bed. "Goodbye. I'll come again this evening."

Even as she nodded, Lillian's eyes fell shut and her mouth dropped open to emit an un-Lillian-like snore.

The doctor told him the heart attack was a mild one, a warning that Lillian needed to eat a healthier diet, get more exercise, and take the medications she'd been resisting because they were "for old people."

Lillian wasn't much over sixty, Morgan reminded himself on the drive back to the condo. She'd be fine, easily live another twenty years. Long enough to see Joey graduate from college. Harvard, of course, if it was up to Lillian.

"Thompsons and Danbys have always gone to Harvard," he could almost hear her say.

Except Joey wouldn't be a Thompson or a Danby. Unless . . .

His mind flooded with sunny pictures of a future, where he was Joey's father, Rosalie's husband. Baseball at Fenway Park, summers at the house in the Berkshires, weekends on the Cape. Two more children floated through the images, a dark-haired boy who tagged along after Joey, a sassy, smart little girl with Rosalie's eyes. An impossible future.

Rosalie didn't want to move to Boston.

More to the point, she'd laughed when he asked her to marry him.

The memory shot through him, so sharp he wondered why he didn't bleed.

He drove into the garage under the condo building, parked,

and sat there, frozen in place by the realization that he loved Rosalie Walker. Had been in love with her for weeks.

The truth was supposed to set you free, but he only felt more tied up by all the emotions he'd fought long and hard to avoid. Love, but so many others too.

He'd been in a rage last night. No. Another truth—he'd been hurt. And because of it, he'd refused to listen to Rosalie's apologies for not trusting him. Now he didn't need them. He saw as clearly as the California sunshine spilling in through the skylight that she'd been right.

She'd had no reason to trust him. That bit of truth burned like fire in his gut. All he'd done since they'd met was lie and manipulate her.

Yesterday he'd meant to start over, but he'd hadn't told her so, hadn't given her any reason to believe it was anything more than another ploy.

And instead of honestly discussing what Lillian had done and how he felt with Rosalie, he'd shut her out, the way he had his mother all those years ago.

Which left one question—what could he do to earn another chance at a lifetime with the woman he loved?

Chapter Twelve

After a month with no word from Morgan, Rosalie had learned more about the downside of romantic love than anyone should have to know.

She'd learned a broken heart kept right on beating. She'd learned having a toddler around made it impossible to mope, no matter how unhappy you were. At least during the day. At night she was free to torture herself with memories and dreams of what might have been.

She'd learned early on that one face of love was the fierce, primal love she felt for Joey, even though she hadn't given birth to him. The love she felt for Morgan was primal, too, a full-on bliss that still lingered under all the hurt.

She'd wondered at first how she could keep going without Morgan when the mere thought of losing Joey made her mind go blank with pain. Eventually she figured out, Joey needed her. Morgan's continued silence was proof he didn't need her. He clearly didn't love her.

She'd also relearned the helpful lessons her mother's illness had taught her. Focus on the job and the people in front of you. Have short-term goals so something good happens every day. Have long-term goals so you always move forward.

The sadder lessons, too. Men leave. Grief fades.

This new emptiness in her life would fade too. After all, she had everything she wanted—the adoption was on track, her practice was thriving, and once she got her mother's studio cleaned out, she'd have a real office at home. Then she'd be able to have more work-at-home days with Joey.

Because she'd also learned somewhere along the way that the love she felt for her mother would always be part of who she was, but it was time to make the house hers. Hers and Joey's.

It took a whole weekend to clear out her mother's studio. The next Saturday she invited Vanessa and Aaron over for a pizza-and-redecorating party.

"I'm glad to see you've moved on," Vanessa said as she held one end of the pale-green shade Aaron was almost finished installing over the high windows.

Rosalie looked up from connecting the modem. "Moved on from Morgan, you mean?"

Her friend rolled her eyes. "Moved on from your mother's death. You've been stuck in neutral for a long while now. I thought maybe getting custody of Joey might knock you back in gear, but I guess enough time hadn't passed."

Rosalie opened her mouth to protest, but maybe Vanessa was right. More to think about during the long, sleepless nights.

When Aaron finished with the shade, Vanessa stretched and pointed to the paintings lined up along one wall of the office. "What do you plan to do with those?"

"Sell what I can, keep the rest. Which reminds me, I need to call that gallery." Rosalie turned on the computer, gratified when it lit up at once. "Do you guys want a painting?"

"Your mom gave us one as a wedding gift," Aaron reminded her.

"It was an engagement gift," Vanessa corrected. "Rosalie's mom knew she probably wouldn't be there for the wedding."

"Oh, yeah." Before Aaron could add an apology Rosalie didn't want or need, the doorbell rang. "Pizza's here!"

Once they'd finished eating, Rosalie took advantage of having her friends around to keep Joey entertained and called the gallery. She was surprised the woman who answered the phone put her immediately through to the owner.

"I had it on my calendar to contact you next week," he told her. "We've sold all of your mother's paintings we have and I'm sure we can sell more."

Rosalie smiled at the chance to add to Joey's college fund. Her mother would be pleased.

"When can you come by and look at them?"

She heard the click of computer keys. "Wednesday afternoon? Or evening? Around seven? You work days, don't you?"

"Wednesday evening is fine. I'll see you then."

"Er, no, I'll send an associate."

Probably the woman who'd answered the phone. "Oh, okay. Thank you again."

She put the time on her calendar and went back to join the others in the dining room.

By six-thirty Wednesday evening, Rosalie was exhausted. She'd had a bankruptcy hearing in the morning and a tearful, newly separated wife in her office most of the afternoon. The last thing she wanted now she'd gotten Joey home and fed was to deal with the woman from the gallery, but it was way too late to cancel. She shook off the gray mood of the day the best she could and took Joey across to Mrs. Peterson's.

The woman from the gallery would undoubtedly be dressed like someone out of a magazine, but Rosalie didn't have the time or energy to work any miracles. She threw a clean blouse over the jeans she'd changed into after she got home from work and did a minimum with her hair and makeup.

The doorbell rang right on time, almost as if the woman had

waited outside for the precise hour. Rosalie double-checked the array of paintings spread across the dining room, the living room, and her new office before she went to open the door.

Morgan stood on her front step with the strings to a dozen golden balloons in one hand and a single pink rose in the other. In a dark suit and blue shirt he looked like a picture from a magazine. A picture from her dreams.

"You!" She started to close the door, but he held the rose out to her.

Maybe it was the bleakness in his eyes. Maybe it was the burst of mad delight in her heart when she first saw him. Whatever the reason, she was weak enough to take the flower.

"The lady at the flower shop said a pink rose means 'please believe me.'" His tone was casual, despite the lines of tension around his mouth and eyes.

As the first shock faded, a wave of pure rage washed away any softer emotions. How dare he show up now, when she'd begun to believe that someday she might get over him?

Before she could slam the door in his face, a movement in the corner of her eye warned her that the cats were on the verge of another escape attempt.

Morgan took advantage of the distraction to quickly step through the door and shut it behind him to block their way. "Sorry, guys."

The cats flicked their tails and slunk in tandem into the living room.

Rosalie ignored Morgan's teasing smile and glowered at him.

"What do you want? Did Lillian send you?"

"No. She's gone to Maui to adjust to the idea she's not twenty-five anymore."

Maybe because she'd been thinking about Joey's college fund, Morgan's casual comment made her realize for the first time that Joey might never need the money she'd put away for him. Someday, he'd be a very rich man. And her job was to make sure he knew how to cope with the sudden wealth.

Morgan looked at the paintings set out everywhere. "Is there any place we can sit and talk? Or would you rather do this here?"

"Do what?"

"Have me grovel."

The image of Morgan Danby at her feet made Rosalie laugh in spite of herself. He frowned for a moment, then smiled that sexy smile.

"Try not to drool on my toes," it gave her the courage to say. "I just had a pedicure."

Morgan closed his eyes and grasped the balloon strings wrapped around his hand so tightly they bit into his flesh. "Tell me your toenails aren't red."

Rosalie laughed again. "Purple."

He groaned and opened his eyes, but his witty reply died in his throat.

She'd remembered she was mad at him. She stood with her arms crossed over her chest while her eyes shot angry bolts at him.

"What do you want?" she asked again.

"To talk to you."

He watched in muted panic as her scowl deepened.

"I have good news about the adoption," he added.

Her rigid posture softened a bit. He let out the breath he'd been holding.

"Come in the kitchen," she said. "I need to get this flower in some water. We can talk in the breakfast room."

Not the warm invitation he wanted, or the atmosphere he would have chosen, but beggars couldn't be choosers. He winced at how apt the old saying was.

She bent over to dig a vase out of a bottom cupboard. The pull of her jeans over her rounded backside sent hot shivers of need through him, but he knew sex had to be way down the road. If there was any sex in their future at all.

He turned away to tie the balloons to the back of Joey's highchair, then sat at the round table in the nook. Rosalie put the rose in a tall, narrow vase and set it on the table. She settled in the chair across from him, her face unreadable.

"So, what's this good news about the adoption?"

"Before we go there, I want to thank you for convincing the police that what happened with Lillian was a misunderstanding. She got off without even an arrest on her record."

Not something his stepmother appreciated at first, but he'd worked hard to drive home to her what could have happened if Rosalie had let the legal process take its course.

"I don't want to ruin her life. I just want her to go away and leave us alone."

"Well, she'll always be Joey's grandmother, but . . ." He reached into his pocket, took out the carefully folded papers, and laid them on the table in front of her. "The top one is a notarized letter from Lillian surrendering any claim to custody of Joey." Rosalie's gaze lifted from her lap to his face. "The other one relinquishes all Charlie's parental rights."

Rosalie banked the flare of delighted surprise in her eyes.

"Charlie killed Joey's mother," she said. "I could have gone to court to force him to relinquish, if I needed to."

"I know, but now you don't have to." Morgan leaned closer, gratified when she didn't pull away. "You don't have to do everything on your own anymore."

She did stiffen at his words, the small movement another twist to the tension in his heart.

"Thank you." Her neutral tone told him nothing.

"Don't thank me. I should have done this a long time ago, as soon as I knew Joey wasn't stuck in foster care somewhere but was in a secure, happy home with someone who loved him. But I was so mad that you'd tried to trick me, I let my pride get in the way and told Lillian I'd found him. If I'd done the right thing in the first place, none of this would've happened. I'm sorry I acted like such an arrogant jerk."

"You are an arrogant jerk. Or you can be. But I'd have had to contact your stepmother before I adopted Joey in any case."

"But you would have had me on your side."

She frowned. "Now you mention it, you did act like an arrogant jerk—you came to my office, demanded information, tried to manipulate me by pretending to be attracted to me . . ."

"I am attracted to you," he interrupted. "But you're right, I used the physical chemistry between us to try to get you to play along with my plan and marry me."

"A plan you could have told me about. I would still have refused to marry you, but maybe together we could have come up with a better plan."

"Frankly it never occurred to me to just talk to you," he admitted. "That's not how I learned to deal with women, outside of a business context."

"Your father and Lillian's marriage must have been interesting to watch," she muttered.

He shrugged. "Their marriage was better than my parents'. That one was a battlefield." Words he'd never meant to say pushed themselves out. "I was the collateral damage. I hated living in a war zone." He swallowed. "Hated it so much that when my mother came to say goodbye before she left, I told her I hated *her*. I haven't seen her since."

The room went very quiet. He stared down at the table, unable to look at Rosalie or anything in the house that declared in a thousand ways how much she'd loved her own mother.

"It must have been hard for you," she finally said.

Before he could do more than blink in disbelief, she pushed her chair back.

"I need a cup of coffee. Would you like some?"

He'd like a stiff drink, but he'd take what he could get. "Thanks."

180

He stayed where he was, calmed by the homey sound of her movements in the kitchen and the fact that she hadn't tossed him out on his ear after his little revelation.

The bittersweet aroma of dark-roast coffee filled the air.

"I won't get any sleep tonight after this," Rosalie commented as she put the mugs down on the table and sat back down across from him.

He didn't want to ask if she meant the coffee or the conversation.

She took a sip from her mug before she knocked his legs out from under him.

"You never did tell me why Lillian let her ex have custody of Charlie."

A chasm opened up in front of Morgan. He'd already told her things he'd never confessed before. He still didn't have any idea where all this was headed, but if he stayed where he was, on the safe side of the chasm, it wouldn't go anywhere he wanted to be.

Morgan felt the same terror in his throat he had as a kid. It was bad enough he'd driven his own mother away . . .

Except he hadn't. That was how he'd made sense of what happened when he was six. He knew better now. He'd known better for a long time. Now he'd confessed what he'd done to someone else for the first time, he knew it in his mind and in his heart too. But Rosalie wanted another piece of truth, one he'd buried even deeper.

His right hand clutched his upper left arm. The risk of emotional pain ahead blended into long-ago physical pain.

At nine he'd hidden the pain to keep the closest thing he had to a mother in his life. To keep Rosalie in his life, he'd have to bare it all.

"You know how Charlie is." Involuntarily, he rubbed his arm. "He always liked to have a human punching bag handy. Black eyes, bruises, a broken nose weren't enough. It took a broken arm and a midnight trip to the emergency room to pull my father's attention away from Danby Holding. At dinnertime the next day, in front of me and Charlie, he gave Lillian an ultimatum. Either she turned custody of Charlie over to his father or my dad would throw them both out."

The look on Rosalie's face told him she'd already suspected some of what he'd told her. Her empathy made it easier to finish.

"Lillian made the only choice she could have, being Lillian. She sent her son to Paul Thompson to raise rather than lose the wealth and status she had as my father's wife."

Rosalie let out a long breath. "I'm sorry you went through all that."

"It was a long time ago."

She raised one eyebrow and nodded at the hand still clutching his arm. He lowered the hand to his lap and took a long drink of coffee.

"So," she said after a long pause. "If you had good news, why didn't you call and say, 'Hey, I'd like to drop by?'"

"Because I wasn't sure I'd be welcome." Her wary expression pushed his tension up another notch. "I wasn't even sure you'd answer your cell once you saw my number."

"So you just show up, knowing it would be harder for me to throw you out if you took me by surprise. You can add tonight to your arrogant-jerk power plays."

"I'm sorry." He hesitated. "Do you want to throw me out?" His heart froze, but he kept his face neutral.

"I'm not sure." She turned away to touch the rose again. "What did you say the rose meant?"

"Please believe me."

She nodded, eyes still on the rose. "Believe you about what? It was obvious the moment we got to Lillian's hotel room that night that you weren't in on her little plot."

He shook his head. "I want you to believe I'm sorry I got angry when you thought I'd helped her. I understand now I hadn't given you any reason to think otherwise. I should at least have let you apologize, although you really didn't need to. But I couldn't get past the feeling that if you believed, even for a moment, I'd want to take Joey away from you after what we'd shared, we didn't have any future together."

"Do we have a future together?"

That was the real question here. Rosalie had thought her heart couldn't hurt anymore after she'd sat through Morgan's heart-breaking story, but she'd been wrong. It pounded wildly in her chest in protest as the silence between them grew longer, thicker.

In the end, she was the one to break it. "Or did you come by for some hot, easy sex?"

He swore.

"I asked you to marry me," he reminded her.

"So Lillian could be near her grandchild."

"So I could spend the rest of my life with you."

Her heart in her throat, she fought to stay angry. To stay safe. "Okay, a lifetime of hot, easy sex."

"Nothing is easy with you." He stood and paced the length of the kitchen and back. "Why do you have to be so dumb now when you're so damn smart the rest of the time?"

"Dumb about what?"

"The rose, for starters. I thought you'd understand flowers."

"It's gorgeous. Thank you. But . . . well, I have a garden full of roses."

"Planted by your mother." The edge of exasperation in his voice surprised her.

"Roses, flowers, were part of nature for my mother. Colorful, graceful shapes she shared with others in her paintings. She didn't care what meanings people associated with them."

"Ah." He paused in the kitchen door and stared into the dining room full of canvases.

A new suspicion drifted into her mind. "Is your friend who

owns the gallery really interested in more of Mother's work, or did he say he was to help you?"

"No, he says he can sell whatever you have. I'm supposed to bring the whole lot over to the gallery tomorrow."

"I've put the money away for Joey's college, but I realize now he may not need it."

Too much information. Her worry over how Joey would handle his future wealth had taken advantage of having someone to share it with and slipped out before she could stop it. She didn't want Morgan to think she cared about Lillian's money. Or his.

But all he said was, "It depends on how much you let Lillian be part of Joey's life."

"I don't plan to shut her out completely, if she behaves herself."

"That's kind of you."

A silence fell. He didn't make any effort to fill it, and neither did Rosalie. She was too focused on the need to fight the almost physical pleasure at having Morgan standing in her kitchen as if he belonged there, the tingle of sexual excitement from his nearness.

When the refrigerator cycled on they both jumped.

"Is any room in this house not full of paintings?" he asked.

"Just the bedrooms."

Definitely too much information. A wolfish smile spread across his face.

But he shook his head. "We cannot have this conversation in a bedroom. Talk first, sex later. I've learned that much."

She stiffened, as much a defense against the lure of surrender as a response to his words. "I don't remember mentioning sex."

"You accused me of coming here for hot, easy sex."

Heat crept up her face. "I can't see any other reason for you to come all the way to Los Angeles. You could have told me about these," she tapped the papers, "in an email."

He paused. Her heart paused too, and her breath froze.

"I came here to grovel. And to ask for a second—or is it a third?—chance."

She kept her face calm, but her body roared back to life. Flutters of hope, need, desire flowed from her head to her heart to her core and back again.

"You give good grovel," she admitted. "I've lost track of how many chances it is, so one more probably won't hurt."

His face remained calm, but some of the tension flowed out of his body.

"What do you intend to do with another chance?" she asked him.

"I could call and say 'Hey, I'd like to drop by,' except I'm already here."

He came to her and reached out his hand. Hers went into it naturally. The contact was sweet, solemn, with an undertow of need that silenced them both.

She cleared her throat. "We could move the paintings to your car."

"And then . . .?"

"We could go into the living room and you could grovel in comfort."

His mouth tilted up in a smile that crinkled his eyes. His oh-so-sexy mouth. His sex-on-the-beach eyes.

Before she gave into an impulse she'd probably regret, the cats wandered in and sat at Morgan's feet, furry reminders of real life. She pulled her hand free.

"You put the paintings in the car. I'll go get Joey. Mrs. Peterson only agreed to keep him for an hour or so. She's got a TV show on tonight she refuses to miss."

Morgan wasn't sure whether Joey's presence would help his cause or hurt it, but he didn't have much choice in the matter. He moved the larger paintings to the back seat of the BMW sedan

185

he'd rented and arranged the smaller ones in the trunk. Rosalie threw on a

jacket and disappeared across the street. She came back with Joey and waited while Morgan closed the trunk with a solid, but almost silent, thunk.

The moment Joey saw Morgan, he lifted his arms toward him and cried, "Mawg!"

Helpless in the face of the boy's grin, Morgan took him from Rosalie and let the boy wrap grubby hands around his neck to lay sticky kisses on his cheek.

A wave of some fierce emotion washed over Morgan when he held the boy's warm weight against him. No one and nothing could ever be allowed to hurt this child.

"I'm surprised he remembers you," Rosalie commented as they walked up the front path.

"Hey, don't underestimate the step-uncle/step-nephew bond."

"Yeah, sure."

She opened the door and took Joey from him. The kid muttered a drowsy protest.

"You want to watch me get him ready for bed?"

The simple ritual of bath, diaper change, pajamas brought Morgan a rush of new emotions for both mother and child—soft, sweet, and infinitely tender.

He'd never expected to love Charlie's child.

He'd never expected the far more passionate love he felt for Rosalie.

Joey fell asleep as soon as she tucked him in. Morgan gave the child's tummy one last pat before he pulled himself away from the serenity of the moment.

Rosalie took her mug to the living room, unsure what to say or do. Morgan's gentleness with Joey had revealed a side of the man she loved that she hadn't let herself believe existed.

"Wait there." He disappeared into the breakfast room and

reappeared with the strings to the balloons and his mug in one hand, the rose in the other.

Delight rippled through her, just as it had when she first saw him at her door.

He tied the balloons to the arm of the broken chair to keep them away from the cats, and set the vase and mug on the coffee table while she settled on the sofa. He sat next to her and took her hand, fueling all the little fires inside her she fought so hard to keep under control.

Maybe she didn't need to fight anymore. Maybe she didn't need to be alone anymore.

She moved her hand against his and the little fires became ribbons of hot hunger woven through her body and knotted at her core.

"What comes next?" she asked, to hide her reaction. "More groveling?"

He touched his fingers to each other as if counting something.

"Do I have anything left to.apologize for?"

"I think a good grovel should include a pledge to do better in the future."

He lifted her hand to his lips. "'Arrogant jerk' isn't strong enough for what an ass I've been. You'll need to help me be a better man. You'll have to teach me honesty."

He took her other hand and lifted both to his lips for a quick kiss. Her heart drummed madly at the adoration in his eyes.

"The balloons mean I love you."

Her heart stopped. Time stopped.

She closed her eyes to hold the words closer.

"I love you, too."

He gave a start. "Sometimes—lots of times, I didn't think you even liked me."

Not quite the response she'd hoped for, but his honesty demanded her own. The honesty she'd always prided herself on, but had somehow lost since she met him.

"I don't go to bed with men I don't like."

"Ahh. So I should have known all along?"

"You should have known what kind of woman I am."

"You're hard to know. Too many layers. I feel I could spend my whole life with you and never know everything about you."

She let herself smile. "Maybe that's a good thing."

"Maybe it is."

She would never be sure who moved first, but the next instant they were in each other's arms. His kiss was tentative at first, but she licked his lips and, with a moan, he claimed her mouth with an unmistakable passion. She sank deeper and deeper into the warmth and strength of his body, the fiery desire of his kiss, while her heart and soul soared with joy.

She could have spent the rest of her life right where they were, but he finally pulled away with obvious reluctance.

"Rosalie?" His voice was rough and a hint of red colored his face. "Will you marry me?"

The explosion of joy left her mind blank, but she heard herself say, "Yes."

"Just yes? No 'where will we live, where will I work'? Are you sure you understood the question?"

"No." His confused expression made her smile. "I mean, yes, I understood the question, but I know you well enough now to trust you've come up with a plan that will make us both happy. You're good with plans."

"You don't you want me to swear I want to spend the rest of my life with you?"

Her heart bounced with joy, like the bouquet of golden balloons he'd bought her.

"You don't want to hear how I've arranged to move the head-quarters of Danby Holding Company to Los Angeles to make a place for you and Joey in my life? At the center of my life."

She swallowed tears of happiness as he pulled a small box out of his pocket and opened it. The large, round-cut diamond was set in a circle of small emeralds.

She'd never seen anything so perfect. She held out a trembling hand and he slipped it on her finger. "It's beautiful."

"You like it?"

"You sound surprised."

"It belonged to my grandmother. My mother and Lillian considered it too old-fashioned and wanted new ones specially designed for them."

"I love it. But the ring isn't important. What matters is that we'll be a family now. Forever."

Forever. A word she'd never let herself think before. But it was the right word, the only word for how she felt about this man. And how he felt about her.

Morgan didn't say anything, but stood to sweep her up in his arms and carry her to her bedroom. The magic of the moment silenced any possible protest. She rested her head against his shoulder and let the joy wash over her.

When they reached her room, he slid her slowly down his body. Once her feet were on the floor, he kissed her, then pulled back.

"I've never done this with a kid around before."

"Neither have I. But he's asleep."

"What if he wakes up? What if he gets out of the crib?"

She gave him a smile, crossed the room, and locked the door with a loud lick before she returned to his arms, eager to celebrate their love with the pleasure only this man could bring her.

Acknowledgements

First of all, I'd like to thank my critique group – Ellen Lindseth, Lizbeth Selvig, and Laramie Sasseville/Naomi Stone – for their keen insight and endless support.

Thanks, too, to my agent, Scott Eagan, who always helps me write a better story, and my editor, Charlotte Ledger, the one who took a chance on me.

I'd also like to express my appreciation to the Romance Writers of America and my local chapter, Midwest Fiction Writers, for providing the community of writers that keeps me going.

Thank you to my two grown children, who don't understand why I do this, but get excited about my successes anyway.

Finally, a thank-you to my hometown, Los Angeles, for inspiring this book.